Yo...

Privileged

Woman.

INTRODUCING

PAGES & PRIVILEGES™.

It's our way of thanking you for buying
our books at your favorite retail store.

— *GET ALL THIS FREE* —

WITH JUST ONE PROOF OF PURCHASE:

◆ **Hotel Discounts** up
to 60% at home and
abroad ◆ **Travel Service**
- Guaranteed lowest
published airfares
plus 5% cash back
on tickets ◆ **$25 Travel Voucher**

$50 VALUE

◆ **Sensuous Petite Parfumerie** collection

◆ **Insider Tips Letter**
with sneak previews
of upcoming books

*You'll get a FREE personal card, too.
It's your passport to all these benefits– and to
even more great gifts & benefits to come!*

There's no club to join. No purchase commitment. No obligation.

Enrollment Form

☐ *Yes!* I WANT TO BE A *Privileged Woman.*

Enclosed is one *PAGES & PRIVILEGES™* Proof of Purchase
from any Harlequin or Silhouette book currently for
sale in stores (Proofs of Purchase are found on
the back pages of books) and the store cash
register receipt. Please enroll me in *PAGES
& PRIVILEGES™*. Send my Welcome
Kit and FREE Gifts -- and activate my
FREE benefits -- immediately.

*More great gifts and benefits to come like these
luxurious Truly Lace and L'Effleur gift baskets.*

▼ DETACH HERE AND MAIL TODAY! ▼

NAME (please print)
_____

ADDRESS _____ APT. NO _____

CITY _____ STATE _____ ZIP/POSTAL CODE _____

PROOF OF PURCHASE
SAMPLE ONLY
Pages & Privileges™

Please allow 6-8 weeks for delivery. Quantities are
limited. We reserve the right to substitute items.
Enroll before October 31, 1995 and receive
one full year of benefits.

NO CLUB!
NO COMMITMENT!

*Just one purchase brings
you great Free Gifts
and Benefits!*

(More details in back of this book.)

Name of store where this book was purchased_____

Date of purchase_____

Type of store:

☐ Bookstore   ☐ Supermarket   ☐ Drugstore

☐ Dept. or discount store (e.g. K-Mart or Walmart)

☐ Other (specify)_____

Which Harlequin or Silhouette series do you usually read?

_____

Complete and mail with one Proof of Purchase and store receipt to:

U.S.: *PAGES & PRIVILEGES™*, P.O. Box 1960, Danbury, CT 06813-1960

Canada: *PAGES & PRIVILEGES™*, 49-6A The Donway West, P.O. 813,
North York, ON M3C 2E8

PRINTED IN U.S.A

"Have You Forgotten What An Awful Pest I Was? You Could Hardly Turn Without Tripping Over Me."

"Was that you?" Jeb grimaced in mock surprise. "I thought it was my shadow."

"Sure, with wild, shaggy hair and glasses perched eternally on the end of her nose. *Its* nose."

Jeb reached across the table to slide a finger beneath a lock of hair, tucking it behind her ear as he'd seen her do. He remembered when he used to ruffle it to a tousled mass. Now it was sleek, smooth, silky to his touch.

"I have to admit I never knew what a shame it was to hide this under those heavy glasses. And your eyes? You can't expect me to believe I'm the first man to tell you how wonderful they are."

"Contacts."

"No, Nicky, not the contacts. Your eyes. *You.*"

Nicole tried to take back her hand. He refused to let her go, holding her fast as he leaned back in his chair, looking at her as a man would look at a beautiful woman.

As she'd always wanted him to look at her.

Dear Reader,

Imagine that you're single, and you've been longing for a family all your life...but there aren't any husband prospects in sight. Then suddenly, a handsome, sexy rancher offers you a proposition: marry him. The catch— you've got to help raise his four rambunctious children. It's tempting...but is it practical? That's the dilemma faced by Kara Kirby in this month's MAN OF THE MONTH, *The Wilde Bunch* by Barbara Boswell. What does Kara do? I'm not telling—you have to read the book!

And a new miniseries begins, MEN OF THE BLACK WATCH, with *Heart of the Hunter* by BJ James. The "Black Watch" is a top-secret organization whose agents face danger every day, but now face danger of a different sort—the danger of losing your heart when you fall in love.

In addition, the CODE OF THE WEST series continues with Luke's story in *Cowboys Don't Quit* by Anne McAllister. And the HEART OF STONE series continues with *Texas Temptation* by Barbara McCauley.

For a light, romantic romp don't miss Karen Leabo's *Man Overboard;* and a single dad gets saddled with a batch of babies in *The Rancher and the Redhead* by Suzannah Davis.

I hope you enjoy them all—I certainly do!

Lucia Macro
Senior Editor

Please address questions and book requests to:
Silhouette Reader Service
U.S.: 3010 Walden Ave., P.O. Box 1325, Buffalo, NY 14269
Canadian: P.O. Box 609, Fort Erie, Ont. L2A 5X3

BJ JAMES
HEART OF THE HUNTER

SILHOUETTE *Desire*®
Published by Silhouette Books
America's Publisher of Contemporary Romance

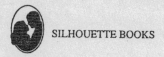

SILHOUETTE BOOKS

ISBN 0-373-05945-0

HEART OF THE HUNTER

Books by BJ James

Silhouette Desire

The Sound of Goodbye #332
Twice in a Lifetime #396
Shiloh's Promise #529
Winter Morning #595
Slade's Woman #672
A Step Away #692
Tears of the Rose #709
The Man with the Midnight Eyes #751
Pride and Promises #789
Another Time, Another Place #823
The Hand of an Angel #844
*Heart of the Hunter #945

*Men of The Black Watch

BJ JAMES

married her high school sweetheart straight out of college and soon found that books were delightful companions during her lonely nights as a doctor's wife. But she never dreamed she'd be more than a reader, never expected to be one of the blessed, letting her imagination soar, weaving magic of her own.

BJ has twice been honored by the Georgia Romance Writers with their prestigious Maggie Award for Best Short Contemporary Romance. She has also received the *Romantic Times* Critic's Choice Award.

AUTHOR'S NOTE:
Although Kiawah truly exists and is as lovely as I've said, perhaps even more so, no ruin lies on its shore. No legend is told of a foolish dreamer who built a castle for his forbidden love. But those who have been to Kiawah will know, and those yet to go will discover, that such a love affair could be much more than fantasy on this enchanting island.

Enjoy,
BJ

One

He watched. From his quiet lair, his hard stare never wavering, he looked down on the shore.

Down at her.

In this hour after dawn, as gulls glided like shadows against the horizon and waves spilled a froth of gold over glittering sand, there was the woman.

Only the woman.

As the sun lifted above the tree line, the sky was alight with a waiting promise of the white, searing heat of a windless day. But for now, as first light turned the massive window where he stood to a luminous canvas, morning clung doggedly to a fragile cool.

Morning on the island, a collage of contrasts. As was the woman who walked in solitude.

The island was Kiawah, a sultry emerald adorning the coast of South Carolina.

The woman was Nicole Callison.

Callison.

He must not forget.

A wordless mutter ruffled a calm steeped in luxury, the low sound of tempered fury and regret echoed hollowly from cavernous heights. In his stark face, rigid lips thinned to a grim line, mirroring a struggle for discipline that could mean his life.

There was no place for anger in this, nor regret. He was the hunter; Nicole Callison his snare. He would do what he must with no recriminations.

None.

Keeping field glasses trained on her, he lifted his first cup of coffee for the day to his lips. Forgotten in singular concentration, it was tepid, as black and oily as diesel fuel. He barely noticed. He waited for the moment when she would turn, when he would see her face. The face of his quarry.

Glasses clenched hard in one hand, nails scoring pebbled leather, he turned in place, moving only as she moved, tracking her path to the ruin hunkered in the sand. As she began climbing slabs of stone stacked helter-skelter like fallen dominoes, he went utterly still. No effort was needed, now, to keep her in sight. Perhaps not ever, for he'd known her ultimate goal. A sheet of broken marble that rested at its pinnacle, the last crumbling vestige of a ballroom where a dreamer called Foley and a woman of mystery danced through the fury of a hurricane as it swept his gift of love away.

What the ancient storm consigned to the sea on that night, the shore had been a half century reclaiming. Now the ruin and its legend stood on shifting sands, an abiding testament of the pomp and grandeur of another time, of courage and frivolity and unmatched devotion. Scoffed at and revered by the islanders and history alike, Foley's castle became Folly's Castle, as it was left as nature would have it.

Folly or masterpiece, there was magnificence in the weather-beaten ruin gleaming dully in the sun. As there must have been in the woman bound to it by love. As there was in the woman who stood drinking in the sight of sea and sky as if there were no more perfect place.

Drawn by the light, defined by it, the line and curve of her body was etched against the backdrop of vast, glittering blue. She was small, five feet two, perhaps three. Beneath the fall of a faded T-shirt her hips were slim, her breasts shapely and free. Legs, clad in tattered shorts just visible beyond the hem of her shirt, were strong and tanned. From bare toes to the battered straw hat tugged low over her forehead, she was the complete beachcomber.

Too complete? he wondered. Through narrowed eyes he studied the subtle sophistication in her bearing, the casual dignity in every move and stride. Was she innocent, or consummate actress? Was there purpose in the role she played? A reason for her quiet existence among the revelers of the exclusive island community?

Why was she the span of a continent from her home, walking the Atlantic shore not the Pacific? What circumstances brought her to trade West for East?

Was she running? Hiding?

Waiting?

Waiting for what? For whom?

The cup he'd forgotten thudded to the table at his knee. Only half aware he'd set it aside, or that he'd caught his breath again, he watched as she faced the shore at last.

There was no elegance now, no sophistication, only the naturalness of a woman at ease with her world. With a sudden fling of her hand, her hat was spinning over the sand, the flamboyant scarf tied at its crown fluttering like the tail of a playful kite.

A shake of her head sent her close cropped hair flying and shimmering in the sun, as iridescent as the wing of a raven. He saw then, as he knew he would, as he had before, that her features had been sculpted kindly by time. Hollows and shadows of maturity made real a beauty that had been a covenant of youth. Her full lips were parted in laughter. Her nose was straight, unmarred by the scar at its bridge. Her eyes were green, sometimes gray or blue, their hue changing with the color she wore.

Today her shirt was red, fading to pink. Her eyes would be green, and were looking directly at him.

He knew it was illusion, a trick of the light. The house with the sun behind it would be no more than squares and angles in black relief against the sky. There was nothing to draw her attention to the sheets of glass that served as doors and windows for the multilevel house. Nothing that would betray him. She had no reason to suspect field glasses, carefully shielded from any telltale glare, tracked every minute detail of her morning ritual day after day. No reason to suspect this quiet routine was intimately familiar to an intruder who watched and waited.

An intruder who stared at her, lost in thoughts of another time, not truly seeing that her eyes were green, nor that the scar curved like a perfect half-moon at the bridge of her nose. For whom that which field glasses weren't powerful enough to discern, and photos from a dossier couldn't relate, memory provided.

This moment came each day, and always with the same effect. The measured beat of his heart thudded harder, his breath shuddered to a halt, and with a sense of déjà vu he stepped back into the past, staring into a face that time had turned to a soft, but perfect replica of another.

The face of Tony Callison, the man she'd worshiped. The man he had come here to kill, if he must.

"And now, Nicole?" The question shattered a pervasive silence. Hoarse from disuse, his voice echoed as before, a hollow sound ricocheting from towering ceilings and bare walls. "Do you worship your brother even now?"

White knuckled and grave, he moved the glasses from his eyes. He stared without seeing sea or shore or woman. His blinded sight turned inward, the coil of doubt he'd fought writhed down his spine. What if she did? What would he do if she knew what her brother had become and was a part of it? How would he deal with what must be done?

Would a split second of doubt cloud his perceptions? Would memory blunt his judgment?

"No!" Denial was fierce and low, more growl than word. Shaking aside an uncommon distraction, he turned from the window leaving the sea to break over the shore unwatched. Leaving Nicole Callison to wander in her solitude. He'd been a hunter too long for sentiment to interfere in his work. A hired gun did what was needed and walked away. This time would be no different.

Tossing the glasses on a chair, he crossed to a telephone. Stabbing out a number he waited for the gruff voice that would need no identification. One ring, two, a third was cut off in midring.

"I've seen enough." He spoke without preamble, lifting his gaze to the window. All that was visible from this vantage was the horizon, where sea and sky blended into one. Listening to the voice on the telephone, he closed his eyes, imagining Nicole Callison sitting atop a tumbled castle by the sea. A siren, unaware, luring the hunted to the trap.

Taking the telephone with him, the coiled cord sliding over tile and carpet as he walked, he returned to the window. With his eyes still lifted to the horizon he nodded absently to reiterated instructions and cautions that needed no answer. When the voice with the hint of a Scots burr was finally silent, he nodded again. "I'll make contact today."

Another rush of instruction crackled over the line. More abrupt cautions. When they were done, the intruder smiled one last time. "Yes, sir, I'll be careful."

A flick of his thumb broke the connection. For a long while he watched the sea changing as the light changed, reflecting the mood of the day. When he looked again at the ruin, she was gone and the early morning had lost its innocence. The first of the promised heat was rising from the sand, marshaling its strength. Soon the temperature would soar, the air would turn sultry. But long before then, when countless sun worshipers dotted the beach with canvas chairs and gaudy umbrellas, she would be hard at work.

So would he.

The first sunbather appeared at the surf's edge as he turned away to make ready for his day. An hour later, when the heat was an inescapable truth, and the shore a milling kaleidoscope of half-naked bodies, he stepped from the geometric extravagance that was his temporary home.

There was no uncertainty in his cold gray eyes, no smile on his lips when he slipped into the roadster parked in his drive. In that rare, unguarded instant he bore little resemblance to the typical islander, the image he'd carefully cultivated among the island inhabitants for weeks.

He was Jeb Tanner, the intruder. The hunter.

No misgivings.

No regret.

The drive to Charleston was uneventful. The bridge spanning the Ashley river afforded a spectacular view, but he was familiar with the coastal city and, today, was unmindful of it. Driving purposefully, and as swiftly as city ordinance allowed, in a matter of minutes he arrived at the entrance of a narrow cul-de-sac. Small shops lined the way, each charming and in complete harmony with the historic atmosphere of the old seaport.

Nicole Callison Galleries lay at the end of the winding pathway.

With a bit of luck and good timing, he captured a newly vacated parking space in an unpaved lot. Sliding the powerful roadster into the narrow space, he was out of the car as the snarl of the engine died. Loose gravel crunched and scattered beneath his feet, roughing the leather of his shoes, but his step was deliberate and sure. The beginning was finally at hand and he was ready to have done with it.

As he passed them by, he squandered no glances on shop windows with ware displayed as works of art. He'd walked the street before. He'd passed them by before. Each time, as now, his attention was riveted on the shop that had only a door of dark wood and leaded glass. A massive door, the final barrier. And Jeb Tanner knew beyond question that when he stepped through it, neither his life nor Nicole Callison's would ever be the same.

At the doorstep, before the nameplate with the gallery hours listed in curling script, he paused. His thoughts drifted to the past as he pondered what he'd been, what a life immersed in secrecy and subterfuge had made of him. And what he would be when this was finished.

A look of irritation crossed his face. He was annoyed with himself, with his questioning. The time for questions was over. He'd come to do a job that must be done, no matter what harm might come to the woman.

The woman. He'd struggled to think of her as no more than that. A warm body, a means to an end, and only incidentally female. She wasn't Nicky. The coltish young girl, who'd tagged along behind her brother and his friend like a lonely puppy, no longer existed.

None of them did, not as they were. The girl had grown into a beautiful woman. Her brother was a brutal murderer who killed as much for pleasure as for greed.

And he had come, bringing the skills he'd been years learning, to end a rampage of terror.

"Whatever the cost."

The brass handle curved against the palm of his hand, bits of glass glinting like rainbows darkened in his shadow, wood swung silently on oiled hinges. A bell jangled a warning peal as he took the step that set into motion a plan months in the making. The door closed at his back and in the cool interior he saw her seated at a desk a little distance away.

The gallery lights were still down. A lamp at her desk spilled a wreath of light over her wrists and hands. For an instant, with her half-averted face bent toward the glowing circle, the years were swept away, and the polished woman was the guileless girl he'd known.

With a rustle, she laid one small canvas aside and another was taken up. He watched as her gaze moved over a mélange of color, recalling a memory of the unwavering concentration of a gifted student ahead of herself in time and place. An innocent, for all her astonishing intelligence, lost and a little confused and with only her brother to cling to.

"Don't stand there by the door rehearsing excuses I won't believe, come on in."

Her voice calling out to him was low, the rich, lilting contralto of a mature woman. He heard the assurance, the throb of stifled laughter, and illusion faded.

"You thought I'd forgotten you, didn't you?" she continued. "I haven't, so stop dawdling and come tell me what you think of these." Intent on the canvas in her hand she seemed unconcerned that her greeting had gone unanswered. "By the way—" her laughter became a chuckle "—good morning."

Wondering who merited the affection he heard in her scolding, Jeb crossed to the desk. As fifteen years slipped firmly back into place, his step became a stalker's step. Light, quiet, undistinguished. The distance was short, a half pace behind her chair he stopped.

She didn't glance away from the simple paintings. "Ashley left these on the doorstep this morning. Before you say it, I know the display is set and including them means rearranging a whole wall. But he's finally agreed to trust us with something of his." Laying a canvas aside, she took up another, tracing the rough edge thoughtfully, as if she would immerse herself in the sun-dappled sea drawn there. "When what he's done is as wonderful as this, how can we not?"

Jeb's cursory glance dismissed the paintings. Not because they weren't moving, or beautiful, but because he couldn't think of paintings now. Not when the woman who had fascinated and intrigued him for weeks was a touch away.

Only a touch.

With her back to him and her head bowed, her close-cropped hair fell in ringlets against the nape of her neck. Like an ebony fringe, it brushed the collar of the fawn colored jacket. Jeb wondered how it would feel to brush away cloth and ringlet and twine his hand about that fragile column. How satisfying to touch her, to capture the warmth of her flesh in his palm, taming the throb of her pulse beneath his fingertips? The need to unravel and understand every facet of this woman was so powerful his arm had lifted, his hand outstretched before he realized what he'd done. For an interminable time his fingers hovered an inch from the curve of her throat.

Like a dash of cold water, reason intruded. To touch her as a stranger would frighten her, and she must not be afraid of him. Not now. Not yet.

Moving back, he listened without hearing. As she rambled on, the scent of jasmine drifted to him. As soft as her voice. As subtle. As lovely.

There was the throb of passion in her, a kindness and innate tenderness. In the half-light he could almost believe she was too guileless to be what he feared. Innocent enough to be the Judas goat he would make of her.

"Look!" she insisted. "Tell me what you think."

Each miniature was accentuated by the lamplight spilling over them, but their glowing colors were only a blur at the edge of his vision. As she waited, silence fell like a heavy curtain.

Sounds of a street coming lazily to life began a distant, whispered chorus. A vendor passed, the wheels of his cart clattering in rhythm with the song of his wares. Soon the life of the street would spill into the gallery and this moment of first meeting would be lost. With an effort, he forced himself to look away from her to the work she offered for inspection. To begin what he must.

"I think you're right." His voice was as low, as husky as hers. "They're very beautiful."

An indrawn breath was cut short. A canvas fell to her desk as she spun to face him. Her hand at her throat and the widening of her eyes spoke her shock as eloquently as her

gasp. "J—?" The incipient recognition was cut short and
rejected in disbelief. With an adamant shake of her head,
she struggled to recover her composure. "Gracious! You
startled me."

"I'm sorry," Jeb said. "The sign by the door says the
gallery is open."

"It does. We are." A flush rushed over her cheeks. "I'm
sorry. We are open, but it's rare that anyone comes in this
early. Except by appointment, of course, and I was expecting my assistant. So, naturally, when I heard the bell I assumed..."

"That I was he, or should I say she?" Jeb finished for
her. He smiled down at her. Beneath the fawn colored
jacket, she wore a lavender frock. A tailored concoction,
fitted like a glove. Her eyes were as gray as a stormy sea.

"She."

"Pardon?" Jeb realized he hadn't been listening.

"She. Annabelle Devereaux. I was expecting Annabelle," Nicole explained distractedly, her face drawn in a
puzzled frown.

"So, naturally, you assumed..."

"That you were..." Her voice drifted to a whisper as she
lost the thread of her conversation. With another exasperated shake of her head, she began again. "Annabelle works
for me and usually she comes in like clockwork, nine minutes late."

She was babbling. Nicole Callison never babbled—it
wasn't allowed. Except, perhaps, she amended, when attractive blond men stood smiling down at her as if she were
the most amusing creature on earth. Which was ridiculous.
The island and Charleston were filled with attractive blond
men. Yet there was something about him, something about
his smile.

With a start, Nicole realized she was staring at him. At the
smile that seemed oddly familiar.

"I'm sorry, ahh..." She looked away from his mouth and
from his captivating gaze. In an uncommonly nervous gesture, her hand lifted to her throat again, to the pulse that
fluttered at its base. "I'm sure you didn't come to hear any
of this." With a visible effort, her gaze returned to his.
"Perhaps there's something I can help you with, something
specific I can show you?"

"No." As she had begun to rise he stopped her with a hand on her shoulder. The contact was electric and startling and over almost as it began, yet the memory would linger. Drawing away, he smiled again. A tighter, less amused version than before. "I only came to browse. I'd prefer to wander about, see what you have to offer." His look ranged over the gallery and returned, deliberately, to her. "Then I'll know how you can help me."

She heard an inflection in his voice she couldn't interpret and saw a subtle difference in the way he looked at her. He was waiting for a reaction, a response to something she didn't understand. Which was as absurd as the entire encounter had been from the beginning. He was simply a customer, albeit from the handsome cut of his clothing and the way he wore it, one of impeccable taste. But, only a customer, nevertheless.

"As you wish." She struggled for the friendly professionalism that was her trademark. Using it as a shield, she brushed her fingers over a panel of digital switches at the side of her desk and the gallery was ablaze with light. A sweep of her hand gave him permission to wander where he would. "Please, look as long as you like. If you have a question, or see something that interests you, my associate should be in shortly and can assist you."

With that, Nicole Callison spun her seat back to her desk, ending any conversation. When he moved away, she gathered up a ledger and to her dismay discovered the entries might be gibberish for all the sense they made.

Still, she tried. Finally, counting it wasted effort, she admitted defeat. Leaning back in her chair, she yielded to impulse and watched him.

As he moved among the displays or paused to study a painting, he appeared quite ordinary. Granted, with broad shoulders and a body that was lean and fit, he was attractive. But no more than others of his sort who had wandered through her gallery. The sea port and the resorts, on islands that dotted the coastline like sandy jewels, drew them like magnets. They came in multitudes, handsome and charismatic, sailors and athletes. Until, by virtue of their number, their uniqueness became ordinary.

Her initial unease, if her reaction could be called that, was simply that he'd caught her unaware. Towering over her as he had, the advantage had been his.

"Advantage," she murmured, not unduly disturbed by her choice of words, or considering it unusual to think of a customer as having a controlling edge. Mollified by the rationalization, Nicole felt a bit foolish when she thought of the hard-bitten look of danger she'd imagined when she first saw him.

First opinions weren't always right, were they? It had to be imagination. Right? If not, why hadn't it occurred to her to be afraid? If he was truly dangerous in his quiet way, why wasn't she afraid now?

Annoyed by the direction of her thoughts, she meant to resolve her nagging questions and dismiss him. Seeking whatever answers had eluded her, her covert stare ranged over him. From shaggy, sun-bleached hair that looked as if it wanted to curl but dared not, to the tips of his leather deck shoes, she inspected him as thoroughly as one would a stallion at auction.

Except she wasn't buying. Not today, and not this one.

As if she'd spoken her disavowal, he looked up from a lithograph. A thoughtful smile teased the corners of his mouth, changing the planes and angles of his features, making them more than pleasant, and much, much more than attractive. And if it destroyed the myth that he was no different from so many others, it strengthened the conviction that any perception of danger in that look and that smile could only be the delusion of a mad woman.

Disconcerted that he'd caught her staring, she nodded curtly. As she resisted the temptation to sink farther into ignominy, a vague frisson of recall tugged at her memory, then flitted away.

Perhaps she was mad, after all, for there was still something about him. Something she couldn't dismiss so easily.

"Nonsense!" The exasperated grumble accompanied a stubborn jut of her jaw as she returned to the work that waited. But work was a poor match for him. As she catalogued paintings and entered them into the ledger, a part of her resisted as another argued he was perfectly innocuous and just a customer. Summoning an elusive discipline she tried to quiet the notion there was anything familiar about him, and attend to the last details of the sale.

Five long, unproductive minutes later Annabelle Devereaux bustled in, her usual good-humored apology and bawdy explanation bursting from her before she realized Nicole was not alone.

"Oops!" She clapped a hand over her mouth, hiding a grin as she looked from one to the other. "Sorry!" she said, and was obviously anything but sorry. "The French libido isn't exactly a proper topic with business afoot, but I didn't realize there *was* business afoot already this morning.

"Wow!" She interrupted herself to lean over the desk. "What are these? No!" She warded off an answer. "Don't tell me." Canvases were shuffled slowly and her grin grew wider.

"Ashley!" Rising on tiptoe to shift a haunch onto the edge of the desk, she rested a stack of canvases on her knee. "You did it! Nicole Callison, you did it! Ashley Blackmon painted these, and somehow you've accomplished the impossible and convinced him to let us show them."

"No," Nicole demurred. "Ashley convinced himself."

"Whatever. I don't care, so long as we have them."

"I'd like to include them in this showing."

"You mean to sell?" Annabelle lifted an incredulous brow.

"Not this time." Nicole shrugged. "Maybe never. Still, I'd like to include them."

"Which means we'll burn the midnight oil to change the exhibit."

"One of us will."

"Wrong!" Annabelle slipped from the desk and straightened her skirt. "Two of us will."

Nicole laughed. "I knew I could count on you."

If Annabelle's grand entrance and conversation commanded Jeb's attention, Nicole's laughter stopped him cold. Before, it had been self-conscious and mechanical. But beyond that, he couldn't remember ever hearing her laugh with such abandon and delight.

As he saw her now, in an element she'd created, speaking with this irrepressible woman who was clearly a trusted friend, he knew he'd never seen her as happy.

When this was finished, when he'd done what had to be done, he wondered what would be left of her life.

"Good morning," a cheerful voice boomed out. "The boss lady suggested that there might be something I can show you."

Jeb turned automatically toward the woman who had appeared at his side. In his millisecond of distraction she'd moved with an astonishingly quiet step after her boisterous entrance. "I'm sorry, I didn't see you there."

"I can understand that. The wolf is beautiful."

"The wolf?"

A dramatic gesture indicated the massive head of bronze where his clenched fist rested. "Since you're two of a kind, it's natural he would be one of your favorites."

At a bit less than five feet, the woman called Annabelle was a foot shorter than he, but what she lacked in height was compensated for by unrestrained flirtation. As their gazes met, hers was flashing, unrepentantly appreciative. His was as aloof as an autumn mist. "I beg your pardon?"

"Honey." Annabelle's eyelids drooped in speculative appraisal. "Any man who looks as good as you, or as bad, has no need to beg anything from me." A hearty laugh bubbled somewhere in the depths of her bosom as her shoulders shook. "At least, not too hard."

"Good and bad?" Jeb mused. "An interesting if peculiar analogy."

"Interesting, maybe. But not peculiar," Annabelle declared. "Not peculiar at all. On the surface you're good-looking in a rugged sort of way, but you can't fool me. Underneath it you're as wild and wily as the wolf, and twice as fascinating."

"Wild and wily?" Jeb was chuckling now. The woman was outrageous and loved every minute of it. "Just an off-the-cuff analysis, huh? And if you had more time, you could delve a little deeper?"

"I wouldn't mind the delving, but it isn't necessary. Any woman worth half her salt can take one look at you and she knows."

"But what does she know?"

A bold look moved over him again. "She knows *everything*."

His chuckle turned to laughter. "I hope not. Sounds dangerous."

"Only for the woman, sugar. But taking a crack at taming you would be worth it." Abruptly her thoughts hopscotched in another direction. "Now that we've settled that, is there something special you wanted to see? Besides the wolf and me, of course."

"Nothing, yet." The words were hardly spoken before he recognized he'd made a tactical error. If he needed to establish himself as a regular and welcome client, he must play what was evidently a game greatly relished by this small person. Play it he would. Teasing her with a look as lecherous as her own, he grinned a lazy grin. The cool gray of his eyes became warm silver. "When I do... need help, that is, should I ask for...?"

As his voice trailed into another tantalizing pause, he saw delight flash in her eyes. Though she was short, shorter than Nicole, and much heavier, the weight was solid and perfectly distributed. With flawless, copper-hued skin and a Gypsy's black mane tousled to perfection, she was a handsome woman. Clearly no stranger to masculine attention.

Indeed, she was handsome, but not beautiful, he decided. Not as Nicole was beautiful.

Keeping his attention focused on Annabelle, he didn't need to glance at Nicole to make comparisons. How she looked had been burned into his brain in his study of her dossier and by weeks of surveillance.

He didn't need to look at her to remember, nor to know that she had abandoned the pretense of working and watched him openly.

"I need to know your name," he reminded Annabelle. "To be sure I get the right woman."

Annabelle's laugh set her bosoms struggling to be free of whatever superstructure confined them. "You are a devil. But you Californians usually are. Always ready to give a woman her comeuppance by reminding her there's other fruit on the tree."

"What makes you think I'm from California?" Jeb was a little alarmed by her astute deduction.

"I don't think, I know. It's the accent. You've been away from it long enough and trained enough that there are only little nuances of it left."

Her allusion to his training was so perfectly on target that Jeb's escalating alarm flickered for a moment in his eyes. For once the little woman seemed blithely unaware and chattered smugly on. "The average person wouldn't hear it, but people come from all over the world to visit Charleston and the islands, and more than a few of them find their way to this gallery. After a while one learns. To be less than modest, I have an exceptional ear for accents and," she added drolly, "it doesn't hurt that I work for a former Californian."

"I'm beginning to think there's a lot about you that's exceptional, Annabelle."

"Annabelle! You devil!" She wagged a finger at him. "You've known my name all along. But how?"

"The boss lady mistook me for you when I came in."

Annabelle's rollicking laugh soared. "That would be a little hard to do."

"Not when there are Ashley Blackmon paintings to distract one."

"That would tend to distract her. At least until she got a good look at you." She leaned closer, lifting her round face to his, to whisper. "Now that she has, she can't take her eyes off you. She's been watching us, you know."

"Is that good or bad?"

"Unusual," Annabelle declared succinctly. "She rarely pays even the handsome ones more than cursory attention. Now." She was hopscotching again. "Are you going to be fair?"

"How so?"

"Running to type, I see." She clicked her tongue and sighed. "Playing the rogue to the hilt."

Jeb grinned. "Comes with the territory."

"I'm sure it does, but are you going to tell me who you are? Or is it that you're a man of mystery on a dark, secret mission?"

The woman was uncanny. He wondered if she weren't the dangerous one. "Sorry to disappoint you, but there's no mystery. As you guessed, I'm a Californian. My name is…"

"Jeb?" Nicole had risen from her seat. Her palm rested on the top of her desk to steady herself. "Jeb Tanner?"

His heart skipped a beat and Annabelle was forgotten as he lifted his head and his gaze met the recognition in hers.

She took a step, then stopped. He saw the need to believe warring with the disbelief written on her face. Gently, surprising himself at how gently, he said, "Hello, Nicky."

"Jeb! It's really you!" Then she was in his arms. Neither would remember later how she got there, only that she had, and that he'd held her close without speaking.

When she drew away at last, her face held a look of wonder. "I thought I'd lost my mind, or that I was dreaming. Then Annabelle said you spoke like a Californian, and everything began falling into place."

She touched his face, brushing his hair with her fingertips. "Why didn't you say something? Why didn't you tell me when you came in?"

"Maybe I wanted to see if you remembered," he murmured.

"How could I forget? I had a horrendous crush on you when I was fifteen."

"But that was also as many years ago."

"Time doesn't matter, a girl never forgets her first crush. Not even a girl who was a nerd."

Jeb caught her hands in his and lifted her fingers to his lips, brushing a kiss over their tips. "You were a smart kid, ahead of herself in time and place. But never, ever a nerd."

"That would've been open to debate." Keeping her hand in his, she looked up at him in unconcealed delight. "Tell me, what on earth brought you here?"

The bell by the door jangled, a trio of chattering women paused only long enough to locate them. "Nicole, my dear, there you are." The eldest of the trio spoke, a haughty summons in her tone. "And Annabelle, how are you, dear?"

"Never fails," Annabelle grumbled under her breath. "The gargoyle always shows up the day before a sale, with her cronies in tow, hoping to get the scoop on everyone else. You two continue as you are, I'll handle her." She patted Nicole's shoulder leaning so close their noses nearly touched. "Don't think I'm not going to hear about this. *Every little detail of it.* You just don't have a rogue like this tucked in your past and keep him hidden. Not without an explanation.

"I'll be back," she promised, and with a swish of her skirt, went to do battle. "Mrs. Atherton" they heard her say, as she waded into the fray. "What secrets have you come to pry out of us today?"

Nicole grimaced at her pointed jab, then smiled a half smile and stepped out of Jeb's arms. "I'm afraid Annabelle misinterpreted this."

"Did she?"

"You know she did."

"So, let her enjoy herself while it lasts." He kissed her hand again, his lips lingering longer than one kiss needed. "We'll set her straight later. In the meantime, I'll let you get back to work."

The bell chimed in another customer.

Jeb lingered, her hand still in his. "We have a lot of catching up to do."

"Yes." Nicole agreed and could think of nothing else to say.

"I could call after the sale."

"I'd like that."

Releasing her, he tugged at a lock of hair that fell over her forehead. "Luck," he whispered as he had when she was fifteen and facing a crucial exam. Leaving her, he went to the door, catching it as a patron entered, sparing them another tinny symphony.

"Nicole?"

"Yes?"

She looked at him with the same unquestioning trust of the coltish fifteen-year-old, and the weight of betrayal crashed down. He could walk away from her and from his mission before that trust was destroyed, but he knew he wouldn't.

"It's good to see you again," he said softly.

As he returned to the street he knew that, no matter what lies he might tell, that much was true.

Two

Jeb stood at the window. Where he'd stood for hours. The shirt he'd pulled over running shorts as he crawled out of bed had been tossed aside. The field glasses, normally a virtual part of his hand, lay on a table halfway across the room. Beside them sat a carafe of coffee, untouched and forgotten.

Beyond the window, his shadowy canvas to the world, the turbulent sea was a caldron of colors, shifting and changing as the rising sun raced to challenge the brewing storm. When he first took up his cold-eyed vigil in the moonless predawn hours, black waves tipped with silver washed over an even blacker shore. Now shades of gold rose out of magenta.

He'd watched each change. From total darkness, to this moment when night met day, he'd noted every nuance with a troubled restlessness.

For the second night he'd tossed and tumbled until, finally counting his quest for sleep lost, he'd abandoned his bed. For the third morning the sands of the shore would be undisturbed by human footsteps.

Nicole's absence, immediately following the sale, came as no surprise. He expected it. From her dossier he knew she kept living quarters in Charleston. A small pied-à-terre, for convenience after tiring late-night sessions in the gallery. For safety, when the drive to Kiawah would be long and desolate. The postsale uproar with its countless details to be addressed would have been such a time.

Two days more had passed. The packing and shipping and additional inventory would be long done, for Nicole worked hard, sparing herself little. Ever. The only indulgence she allowed were solitary morning walks; the only respite, lazy Sundays on the island.

"Sunday." Jeb rapped the window with an impatient fist. "Where is she?"

His growled question was rhetorical. He knew where she was. Hank Bishop, Simon's man in Charleston, had reported where she'd been, what she'd done and with whom, in precise detail. His last report had been that Nicole Callison was tucked safely, and alone, behind her garden wall. That was two days ago. Since then, Bishop had been as silent as the grave.

A second fist rattled the pane as lightning split the distant sky and thunder rumbled. As morning blossomed in new radiance, the darkness churning over the sea had issued its first challenge. But Jeb had stopped thinking of light and darkness and colors.

"Two days." Hands still fisted, he fought a rising impatience. "Two damnable days and nothing!"

Maybe it was the silence that made him too edgy to sleep. Maybe it was that he wasn't accustomed to having a part of his investigations under the jurisdiction of another.

"Maybe it's a lot of things." Bracing against the broad expanse of glass, head bowed, tired eyes closed, his bare chest heaved in a deep shuddering breath. He needed to see her. If she was avoiding him, he needed to know why.

He needed to know now!

Wheeling about without a backward glance at the deserted shore, he went to the telephone. An instrument he trusted little, used only carefully and sporadically, but recently his chief connection to the world outside the walls of his temporary lodging. The number he dialed rang once and, after an eternity, a second time. As Mitch Ryan answered, Jeb went straight to the point. "I'm heading for Charleston."

Mitch Ryan had been his friend for too long, and worked with him too many times to ask why or when or to try to dissuade him. If Jeb Tanner felt the need to go to Charleston, it would be with good reason. If there were circumstances that needed discussion, it wouldn't be over an open telephone line. "All right," the younger man said. "But, in case you haven't looked out your window this morning, don't let this sunshine fool you. There's a mother of a storm brewing out there."

Jeb glanced out the window, really seeing what he'd stared at for hours, and for a moment his world was a polarized void of light and dark. He'd spent the better part of his life on or near the sea, and it never ceased to feel strange to stand in full sun on a beautiful day and watch a squall approach.

From the looks of it, a hell of a squall, gathering strength and staying power. Mitch Ryan and Matthew Sky, two of the best of The Black Watch, had served as his crew more than once before. Water wasn't the natural habitat for a Louisiana street kid and a French Chiricahua Apache, but they'd taken to it like salty dogs.

They were good, better than good, but he was the captain, a sailor born and bred. The sloop and its part in this was his responsibility. "Do you anticipate any problems?"

"Nothing the medicine man and I can't handle." Static crackled over the line and Mitch's voice waffled in and out as lightning flashed again.

"The *Gambler*'s secure?" The sloop, once the *Moon Dancer*, had been heavily damaged in another life. Reworked, repainted and refurbished, then given a new set of papers that wiped out its past, it was reborn as the *Gambler*.

In this mission, Mitch Ryan and Matthew Sky pulled triple duty as Jeb's friends, crew and counterparts. A heavy load, but there was no one whose skill and judgment he trusted more. He could leave everything in their hands. But he had to be sure, and not just about the sloop.

Mitch was a step ahead of him, reading his thoughts, his silence. "The three of us will be safer than you will, Cap. Especially me—I have the medicine man, remember. Monsieur Matthew Winter Sky, the original man who sees things before they're there, and that no one else will ever see. You just worry about yourself, not us. Take it easy on those narrow roads. If you happen to see a pretty girl along the way, kiss her for me."

Jeb laughed then. "You don't need any help in that department, I'll let you do your own kissing."

"Given my limited choices, I think I'll pass. Matthew would knock my head off and the boat has splinters."

A gust of wind swirled about the house and moaned about its eaves. A strafing gull flapped furiously, and sailed backward. Jeb had to go. If he hurried he could beat the worst of what was coming to the mainland. "I'll be in touch."

"You do that. And Cap..."

Jeb waited.

Mitch cleared his throat. Over the scratching telephone line it sounded like a chair scraping over a hollow floor.

Time was precious, but Jeb waited. This wouldn't take long.

Mitch sighed. A vocal shrug of the shoulders to diffuse the depth of what he was feeling, what he wanted to say. Then, "Just watch your back."

"Yeah," Jeb agreed. "Always." With a jab of his thumb the connection was broken and the receiver put down thoughtfully. The conversation was typical Mitch Ryan. No breach of security. No unnecessary questions asked. No unwanted advice given. Tough talk. Teasing names. Levity that fooled no one, then an oblique comment that gave him away if it had.

Mitch was worried, and not about the storm. Tony Callison had gone to ground months ago. He could be surfacing now, in Charleston. The weather would offer perfect cover. And by now he would be desperate, as only a hunted man completely alone could be.

Contradiction sliced though Jeb's thoughts. Not completely alone. He had Nicole. A gut feeling said Simon had been right on target all along. The errant brother would come to his sister. Perhaps, contrary to Bishop's absence of reports, he already had.

Tony Callison might be desperate, and he was dangerous, but he was cunning in the bargain. The man could move in and out of a scene as quietly as a ghost. He'd proven it time and again. Better men than Hank Bishop had been lulled into a false security, thinking the target of his surveillance was too quiet and peaceful to be at risk and in no danger.

When too quiet really meant danger was already present.

"Danger." The word, a constant in Jeb's life, the measure of it, was harsh on his tongue. If the telephone had been in his hand, he would have crushed it. Was Nicole in danger?

In all the hours he'd spent arguing with Simon—resisting this assignment until the absolute end; throughout the exhaustive brainstorming and planning with Mitch and Matthew; in the final stages of pouring over Nicole's dossier— he hadn't wanted to consider that she might become a threat to her brother and, thus, to herself.

Jeb Tanner admitted he'd tried her in his mind long ago and convicted her of one of two crimes. Complicity, or innocent naiveté. He'd nearly convinced himself there were no other choices, and if it came down to it, the lesser crime would protect her. But then he hadn't seen her again. Hadn't discovered the woman the child had become.

Nicole Callison might be guilty as sin, but that sin wouldn't be naiveté.

If Tony came to her with the taint of death clinging to him; if he asked for help, an avenue of escape, a smuggler's ticket out of the country; if she refused him, would he harm her?

Once Tony had loved her too much to let anyone or anything touch her. But that was before.

Before his sociopathic mind lost its last touch with humanity. Before the collegiate bad boy evolved into a conscienceless killer of men and women and, finally, children.

Before the killing became a sadistic ritual, the bounty less important than the pleasure.

Before he became a stalking mad dog, who walked as a man.

If she got in his way, it wouldn't matter who she was, or what she'd been to him. "He would kill her," Jeb muttered, the horror of it, the waste, turning him sick.

Tony would kill her like all the rest.

The image that scorched Jeb's mind sent a shudder down his back. He'd studied the forensic reports and seen the snapshots of what Tony did to his growing list of victims. Each a signature killing, and each worse than the last, until a gruesome pattern of a serial killer began emerging.

"But no more." Jeb's voice was the guttural voice of a stranger, as cold as his eyes. It was the threat of a serial killer with the honed skills of murder for hire that had brought Simon McKinzie and The Black Watch into the pursuit. The same threat had tipped the scales, destroying Jeb's resistance to Simon's plan to trade on his past—renewing one acquaintance to catch another.

With the gruesome facts laid before him, Jeb saw, not the man who had been his rival and his best friend in college, but a monster, potentially more destructive than any the world had ever known. If he were not stopped.

But he would be. And Jeb Tanner would do it.

"Before Nicole's name is on any damn bloody list." If he wasn't already too late.

Dread like cold lead in his belly, Jeb took the stairs in a deliberate pace that ate up the distance more surely than frantic rushing. In the bedroom that occupied the top floor, he slid into jeans, a light shirt and moccasins. A holster was strapped to his ankle and a compact, but powerful, pistol was snapped in it before he gathered up the keys to the roadster. Then he was running down the stairs again, taking them two at a time.

The door slammed behind him on the echo of a single word.

"Please."

The air was humid and fragrant. Shrubs crowded the walled garden walk and the courtyard, their heavy blooms and waxen leaves shimmering like old velvet. In the murky half-light the narrow corridor that bordered Nicole Callison's Charleston home was a magical place of drifting mists and deepening shade, of muted bird song and quiet footsteps.

As she walked through the mist, Nicole reveled in these last minutes before a summer squall. When the wind lay still, city streets outside her gate were wrapped in a waiting hush, and this little part of her world was softer, sweeter. When there truly was peace before the storm.

Soon the wind would rise again, bringing with it the rain, the thunder and the lightning. But when it was done, the city would go on as before, and her garden would be rife with the promise of new life.

Nicole believed with all her being that in Charleston and Kiawah, she'd found the best of both worlds. One offered serenity embodied in a rain-swept garden. The other, the wild exhilaration and the furor of the sea. She loved them both.

She was content with her life. As she wandered this tiny space that was hers alone, she knew she was more content than she had ever hoped. But the way had been long and hard, leading, at last, to a place far away from who she was and where she'd begun. Only then had she put the past behind her.

Three days ago a part of that past had stepped back into her life, and she wasn't sure how she felt about him. She wasn't sure she wanted to feel anything.

Catching a drooping blossom in her palm, she watched as moisture gathering on a creamy petal trembled like tears. The tears she'd shed over Jeb.

Jeb. She'd loved him. With every beat of her fifteen-year-old heart she'd loved him. As she'd trailed behind her brother and his best friend, she'd known his smiles were only kindness, and his kindnesses only pity. But the knowledge didn't keep her from worshiping him.

In the days, weeks and months when classes were a grim, cliquish ordeal, when well-meaning professors singled her out and older students who perceived her as a freak shut her out, there was always Tony. But most of all there was Jeb.

When she was near him, she was even clumsier than usual. All bony knees and jutting elbows. Hair a shaggy disaster. Teeth a mass of silver wires and bands, and her tongue eternally tied to the roof of her mouth. But he never seemed to notice.

"He was just…Jeb," Nicole murmured. He'd been kind and gentle when little else of her life was kind and gentle. Then she loved him even more. For one school year, though he never knew, he was the center of her universe. Then the end of the term came. He and Tony graduated, she became a sophomore. One more rung on the ladder of escape. She'd thought her heart would break without him, and maybe it did, but she'd survived and even flourished in a new life. And she never saw him again.

Until now.

Suddenly she was restless, petals drifted from her hand like falling snow. He had promised he would call after the sale. She wondered if it wouldn't be better if he didn't. She couldn't say why, except that she was afraid. But afraid of what?

The wind stirred, nudged her gently at first, then whipped the full skirt of her dress about her knees, and tangled in her hair. She was glad of the diversion as she hurried to the piazza. She was almost at the first step when a melodic gong summoned her to the garden gate.

"Now who?" she questioned as she retraced her steps over the patterned brick walk. Not a delivery, certainly. Bouquets and gifts wishing her well with the sale would've arrived days ago and at the gallery, not here. Friends and customers had already called in droves, afterward, celebrating her success, until even the most obtuse realized she needed rest and time to herself. Graciously they'd given her exactly that. Time and rest.

So one had decided it was time her self-imposed exile be ended.

Annabelle, of course. Only she would risk a drenching on such a Quixotic mission. Nicole smiled as she imagined the shapely little woman struggling with her voluminous skirt in the wind and weather. But not too hard. Annabelle believed with all her heart that a glimpse of a well-turned ankle, or thigh and maybe a bit of sexy lace was good for the soul. Hers, and what ever kindred souls were nearby. Masculine souls, naturally.

Nicole's amusement lingered as she hurried down the walk that narrowed to a single lane as it neared the street. She hadn't realized before, but, given the turn of her thoughts, Annabelle was exactly what she needed. It was impossible to be moody, or sad or even afraid when she was near.

Lightning flickered overhead. One small flash across a darkened sky, and then another. But long enough to burn the image of her caller into her mind and send it reeling again into the past.

Stopping abruptly a pace away from the gate, Nicole grasped an iron spire as she stared through it to the sidewalk. With graceful spirals and swirls imbued with the strength created by a master ironworker a century before, the gate offered physical protection, but no visual restraint. The man who waited beyond it was clearly visible and unmistakably as handsome as she remembered.

When he smiled at her she was fifteen all over again. With a pounding heart and a tongue that struggled for words.

"Jeb," she managed to say at last. "I didn't expect you." Then, foolishly, "You didn't call."

"No." He shook his head. There were creases across his forehead, from the sun. They weren't there before.

"What are you doing here?" She hated sounding for all the world as if she were still a gawky kid.

"A spur-of-the-moment impulse." Jeb's gaze swept over her windblown hair, the uncertain smile, the simple dress that left her shoulders bare and hid the cleft of her breasts with lace. His gaze moved on, past her to the garden and the shadowed piazza. "Am I interrupting something?"

"Interrupting?" Nicole frowned and brushed a tangle of bangs from her eyes. "No. Of course not. I'm alone. I, uh...would you like to come in?" She was babbling.

Grimly stepping to the gate, with a twist of the wrist she disarmed the lock and drew it back. "Please." She gestured as a sharp gust sent a crape myrtle swaying and scattered scarlet petals over the grass. "Come in before you're soaked."

Jeb hadn't missed the frown, nor the hesitance in her voice. "A little rain won't hurt me, so maybe another time would be better."

If she agreed, taking the excuse he offered, he would have to find another way in. A secret way.

But she didn't take the excuse. Instead, she caught up his hand, tugged him inside. "Don't be silly. I was distracted, that's all. I'm glad you've come. I think it's good that you have."

Jeb's eyes narrowed, suspicion skittered like a serrated knife over raw nerves. But when he spoke his tone was a teasing drawl at odds with the truth. "Do you now?"

"Yes, I do."

A thumb and forefinger at her chin lifted her face to his. He'd looked into this face countless times in the past weeks. He'd seen her smile and laugh. He'd seen her frown. Once, when she'd found a kitten washed on shore from God knew where, he could've sworn he saw her cry. He thought he knew every mood, but he'd never seen her as she was now. Solemn, restive, her eyes fathomless.

Was it fear he saw? Excitement? Danger?

Did Tony Callison wait beyond the gate for him? For both of them?

"Why, Nicky?" he asked, using the name only he had used in the days when they were friends. When he hadn't watched her for any nuance of guilt or warning. When, as now, he'd seen only innocence.

Absently he stroked her chin, a knuckle gliding over skin like pearls. "Tell me," he insisted in a voice as low as a whisper. "Tell me why you're glad I've come."

"Because..." Nicole clenched her teeth, holding back words he mustn't hear. She needed to think, needed to be rational. But she couldn't. Not when he looked at her with such burning intensity that she felt he was trying to see into her soul. Not when he touched her, and his touch was madness.

With a shiver she barely hid, she moved away, and a semblance of reason returned. She couldn't tell him that after spending a weekend hiding from herself and from him, she'd discovered with one glance that hiding was futile. She couldn't tell him that he'd been the love of her young life, and when he left, he'd taken her heart with him. She couldn't in a lifetime tell him how much she'd hurt, and how long.

She couldn't tell him. She'd thought for years that it was all behind her, but now, she wasn't sure. She knew now what she'd been afraid of. What frightened her still—that she would love him again, or that she'd never stopped, and might not survive losing him again.

She couldn't tell him she was glad when she saw him at her gate, because hiding was truly not her way. She was a fighter. No matter how fierce or how frightening, she'd learned to face her problems. Those she couldn't conquer, she lived with in peace.

She couldn't tell him that when he smiled at her, she wondered if there would ever be peace in her life again.

No, she couldn't tell him.

Drawing a long breath, with a wobbly smile, she took his hand. "I'm glad you're here, because you were the best friend I ever had, and I've missed you."

She didn't wait for a reply as she led him down the walk.

With his hand in hers, Jeb went warily with her to her home. Hoping she was as innocent as she seemed, but brutally conscious it could mean his life, if she weren't.

There was caution in every guarded step he took, his darting gaze probing, seeking, finding nothing. The courtyard was small and open and, even filled with plants, it offered no place to hide. Like the courtyard, the piazza was capable of no surprises. The house, a Charleston single, so called because its rooms were arranged in a single row with one opening into the next, was a different matter.

Guardedly, hand itching for the pistol holstered at his ankle, he stepped into the welcoming cool of the first room. The door, another creation of wood and leaded glass, and as striking as that of the gallery, closed at his back with a muted thud. At that moment, as if minding its manners and waiting for a cue, the storm broke with the pent-up fury of a rabid animal.

Ready to move if he must, however he must, Jeb stood barely inside, eyes searching corners of the room and peering through an open door to the next. Watching for shadows that were more than shadow. Listening for sounds of treachery masked by the clatter of rain on the copper clad roof.

Body taut, shoulders rigid, he waited for an attack that never came.

At her look of askance at his stillness, his strange silence, he shrugged and tried to ignore the sweat on his palm, the burning spot in the center of his chest. "Sorry." His lips quirked in a lazy grin, his eyes were flat, watchful. "I was admiring the room. I don't know what I expected, but I like it. It's pleasing, comfortable. You must enjoy it."

That much was true. Nicole had blended antique furnishings with modern, light woods with dark. Another time, under different circumstances, the effect would've, indeed, been pleasing, a comfort when one needed it. Only someone who loved it could have made it so perfect.

"I've read about the Charleston single, its history, the practicality of its architecture, but I've never seen one." He lifted an apologetic brow, as if he were hesitant to ask. But one way or another, he would see the rest of the house. He had to be certain Tony Callison did not lie in wait for either of them. "May I?"

Nicole was bewildered by the request. Jeb's field in college had been history, but he'd been an indifferent student, far more interested in the height of the surf than his studies. But that was a long time ago, a lot had changed, and she knew very little about him now. What he'd done with his life. What profession he'd finally chosen, and what circumstances brought him to the Carolina coast and Charleston.

"Of course." She heard the hint of surprise in her voice, and chided herself that, indifferent or not, history had been his interest, and what place was more deeply steeped in it than Charleston? "This is a typical single, though a bit small if one considers the number of rooms, rather than their size.

At the moment there are only three in use. This one, the bedroom, beyond it a study with bath and dressing room incorporated. The upstairs is storage for the gallery.''

As she spoke, she led him through the house, explaining the lack of closets, the towering ceiling. One room after another, upstairs and down, never more than a pace behind, Jeb rifled her home with his searing gaze.

When the tour was ended, he knew she hadn't lied. She was alone. Tony Callison had not hidden in a murky corner, beneath stacks of stored paintings, nor in the crowded antique chifforobe. Only a mouse could have hidden in the uncomplicated house, and from the gleaming orderliness, he doubted a sensible mouse would be tempted.

"As you've probably discovered, the Charleston single was primarily situated so the doors could be opened to the ocean, to let its breezes pass directly through. In our era of air-conditioning, position wouldn't matter so much." Nicole faltered in her stilted, impromptu lecture. Throughout the tour she suspected he wasn't listening. That his mind was on something else, not the house in which he'd professed such interest. "Jeb, are you sure you really wanted to see and hear all this?"

He smiled down at her, aware that she'd led him back to her bedroom, and that it smelled of jasmine. "I really wanted to see and hear all of it."

Nicole shook her head. This grew more and more curious. He wanted to see, yet he'd been distracted, less intent on historical characteristic than personal. She could almost think he wanted to see the house simply because it was hers. And that made even less sense.

"Why?" She asked the question she hadn't intended. "I mean, I don't understand your interest."

"Don't you, Nicole?" He took her hand in his. Her fingers were slender and smooth. When he had expected nails like rapiers, hers were short and practical. Nails that belonged on busy, useful hands. Hands that toiled.

He wondered if the plants that bloomed in summer's profusion about the house were as much the fruition of her labor as this room. Her bedroom. A woman's room, yet one that would welcome a man and give him comfort.

He wondered, and when he looked into her clear, lovely gaze, he wondered more.

"Does it surprise you that I would want to discover all there is to know about an old friend? What you've done with your life, and why. What you want for the future." His voice sank to a murmur. "When I came to Kiawah, I didn't expect to find such a beautiful woman there. Now that I have, I want to know everything."

"Kiawah?" Her hand convulsed in his. "How did you know I live on Kiawah? In fact, how did you know that I was here?" By here she meant the single tucked so perfectly and unobtrusively in its quiet little alley. He'd walked only by chance into her gallery, yet he knew so much about her.

A slip, Jeb realized grimly. The sort he rarely made, but not as bad as it could have been. Next time he might not be so lucky. Next time he might lose himself completely in that exquisite gaze.

But there wouldn't be a next time. There couldn't.

"I know because I asked," he answered with a casualness he didn't feel. A deceptively straightforward answer that left out who and why. "How better to find you?"

Nicole laughed then. A lot was still unexplained, but for the first time, he sounded almost like the old Jeb. Direct, to the point, never taking refuge in social convention. Truthful to a fault.

She still wasn't sure how she should deal with this handsome fantasy from her past. But, for the moment, she wouldn't deal, she would simply enjoy.

A shutter caught by the wind ripped free and banged against a window. In a whirl of skirts Nicole rushed to the great room in time to see it tumble across the lawn. "Oh, dear. Annabelle will never let me forget this. She'd been reminding me for weeks that I needed to repair that shutter. But with the sale and all it entailed, I never seemed to get to it."

Jeb moved to stand behind her, her subtle perfume filling his lungs as he looked over her shoulder to the courtyard. "Any damage?"

Nicole smoothed her hair behind her ear. "None that really matters. The window didn't break. That's a stroke of luck I don't deserve. It was and, no thanks to me, still is an original set in when the house was constructed during the Antebellum Age. So you see, it survived a great deal. Even my carelessness.''

''I don't imagine you were the first in a hundred years to forget.''

Nicole chuckled. ''No, I don't imagine so.''

Turning, she found herself close to him. Too close. His very nearness took her breath away. He was larger now. Broader, harder. The tensile strength of youth had become the rugged, overwhelming power of maturity.

Strength, power, memories—a heady combination. Dangerous. So dangerous.

Instinctively she lifted a hand to his chest. To hold him away? To brace herself? She didn't know which. She couldn't think. There was only his heart beating beneath her palm.

An unconscious need made her look up, into the face that had changed so much, and yet so little. There were strands of silver in his golden hair, and crinkles around his eyes. But their color was still so like the sea he loved, the dark, rich gray, when the surf would fly.

His skin was weathered, with the look of a sailor's tan. His mouth was . . .

She wouldn't let herself be fascinated by his mouth.

Taking a step back, she gained the space she needed desperately. To breathe. To gather her scattered wits. To calm her jangled nerves. A shaking hand clenched at her side as she struggled for the dignity to play the gracious hostess. Slowly, one long breath at a time, she found the grace. ''I believe I would like a glass of wine, to celebrate an unbroken window.'' Her smile was genial, a little mischievous, and only she knew it was complete bravado. ''Would you join me?''

He wanted to reach for her, to clasp her wrists and bring her back to him, but he dared not. It was too soon, and something had disturbed her. Just when she'd begun to relax, a strange look flickered in her eyes, her wonderful changeable eyes, and she had drawn away.

She wasn't going to be easy. But nothing about Nicole had ever been.

Jeb flexed a tired shoulder, and only then realized how tense he was. Tony Callison was nowhere around, and still he was as taut and grim as death. Was it any wonder she was disturbed? "I'd like very much to join you, Nicole." He returned her smile ruefully. "Maybe a glass of wine is what we both need."

She showed him to a small table that looked out at the courtyard, before folding back the screen that concealed a minuscule kitchen alcove. With nervous moves she collected a decanter and slender goblets, setting them on a tray with a plate of benne seed wafers. The day had been a roller coaster, with one sensation after another tearing at her. When she sat across from him, sipping wine the taste and color of peaches, she was still skittish. Vulnerable.

Vulnerable enough to make thoughtless mistakes, to tell the truth when she meant to lie.

"So tell me, why were you so surprised to see me today?" Jeb turned his glass on the table, his fingers spinning the delicate stem as he watched the undulations of the rosy liquid against crystal. Lifting his head, he met her gaze. "Didn't you know I would come?"

Rain drummed on the roof and dripped from the eaves. Blooms flanking the garden wall bowed drenched heads to the ground. Lightning flashed, turning the courtyard neon bright, and the low lament of thunder faded before she answered. "I wasn't sure you would want to, not when you had time for second thoughts."

"Why wouldn't I?" Jeb took her glass from her, folding her hand into his.

"Have you forgotten what an awful pest I was? You could hardly turn around without tripping over me."

"Was that you?" Jeb grimaced in mock surprise. "I thought it was my shadow."

"Sure, with wild, shaggy hair, and glasses perched eternally on the end of her nose. *Its* nose."

Jeb reached across the table to slide a finger beneath a lock of her hair, tucking it behind her ear as he'd seen her do. He remembered when he used to ruffle it to a tousled mass. Now it was sleek, smooth, silky to his touch. "Nothing this beautiful could ever have been ugly."

"I refuse to show you the photographs that would prove you wrong."

Ignoring her disclaimer, he tapped her nose. "I have to admit I never knew what a shame it was to hide this under those heavy glasses. And your eyes? You can't expect me to believe I'm the first man to tell you how wonderful they are."

"Contacts."

"No, Nicky, not the contacts. Your eyes. You."

Nicole muttered a derisive non sequitur and tried to take back her hand. He refused, holding her fast as he leaned back in his chair, looking at her as a man would look at a beautiful woman. As she'd always wanted him to look at her.

His thumb stroked the rushing pulse at her wrist. There was tenderness in his eyes, and in his smile.

"Friends?" he asked softly.

The rain slowed, then stopped. It was so quiet she could almost believe there was only this. A quiet little world, no fears, no demons. One woman. One man.

Jeb.

Over their linked fingers she smiled back at him, her eyes never leaving his. As softly as he, she murmured, "Yes."

Then she laughed, a happy sound. Perhaps it was because he called her Nicky. Or the outrageous compliments. Or that he'd been kind.

Or even that for no reason at all, she simply wanted to laugh.

Three

Live oaks whispered in the wind. Somewhere across the bay a halyard rapped against an aluminum mast. Ships creaked with the tide, straining against their mooring. The marina had bedded down, the most dedicated reveler long in his bunk. Beneath the familiar clatter a profound stillness gathered in the hours that belonged to the night.

Jeb sat in the darkness, head back, eyes closed, listening to the distant crash of the surf. Below deck Mitch Ryan groused softly to himself as he finished an unexpected chore.

He would have helped with the chore, even welcomed mind-numbing labor. But Mitch had cast an appraising look over him, then said no. And Jeb was left to his thoughts.

Damnable thoughts he couldn't escape.

"Done!" Mitch stepped onto the deck, scrubbing his hands with a cloth reeking of oil. "Good as new." Dragging a match over a brad on his jeans, he stared at its flaring, charring head then dropped it down the globe of a hurricane lamp. In a second he was sprawled in a chair with a groan that welcomed the easing of cramped muscles.

Neither of them spoke as fire hissed and coughed, flickered, then caught the wick in a spurt of yellow flame. The light was a feeble pinpoint beneath a lightless canopy, yet enough that Jeb saw fatigue etched on the younger man's haggard features. The utter weariness his nonchalance couldn't mask.

This little difficulty with the engine hadn't taken long. Not for Mitch. Never for Mitch, who knew engines—cars, boats, any sort—as well as he knew people. The problem was timing, that it had come at the close of a twenty hour day. Jeb suspected there had been and would be more such days.

"Have you slept?" he asked almost to himself, more thoughtful observation than question. "Do you ever sleep, Mitchell Ryan?"

Mitch looked up, his auburn hair stained by sweat. Eyes like sherry, strained and irritated by engine fumes, locked with gray. "Do you, Cap?" His question, as Jeb's, was little more than a thought spoken aloud. "Have you?"

Jeb settled deeper into his chair. After a while he sighed and shrugged. He hadn't slept. He wondered when he would again.

He'd returned from Charleston, then spent the evening searching through Nicole's dossier looking for something he might have missed. Anything that would explain her.

An hour past midnight Simon had called, and his last hope for sleep was gone. Tony Callison had killed again.

A little girl. Thirteen, pretty, quiet. A dedicated student, a long-distance runner training for varsity track. A child much loved, with a lot to live for. Julie, who was never late. Julie, the paradigm of dependability. Julie, too kind-hearted to worry her disabled father. He reported her missing at eight o'clock in the evening, two hours after she should have returned from her daily run.

An hour later a local deputy found her.

Julie Brown was dead.

Word spread. Telephones rang. Julie Brown was news.

Before the avid eyes of the world, tragedy visited the rural midwestern community. Needless tragedy, savage, cruel, the likes of which it had never known. And, if God were kind, would never know again.

Thirteen! The number echoed in Jeb's mind. A knell of sadness for a life hardly begun, ended on a hot summer evening in a shriveling cornfield. A sweet child, tossed aside like a cast-off rag doll, with a cheap, gaudy sun-face medallion draped over a naked, pubescent breast.

The face of the sun. A celestial icon, once the cachet embraced by a close-knit band of surfers. Spoiled and arrogant college kids fancying themselves unique, the self-appointed sons of Apollo, wearing the medallion to prove it.

A symbol of self-centered indulgence and childish narcissism.

Jeb's lay tarnishing in some forgotten box in a dusty attic.

... *when I became a man, I put away childish things.*

But one had not. For Tony Callison this symbol of foolish young men had become a signature for murder.

"Hurts, doesn't it?"

"What?" Jeb jerked back from the black maw of memory.

Mitch glanced at Jeb's clenched hands. "To lose a friend."

"I lost him a long time ago."

"I know." Mitch ignored the bitterness. "But for a while, he was more than just a friend. He was a good friend."

Jeb hesitated, then agreed. "The best." The admission rose out of regret.

"What was he like?"

The sloop rocked with the lazy undulations of the water, a rope scrubbed against a cleat, and Jeb pondered. How did he explain Tony? Could he?

He began with the truth, as he knew it. "Tony could have been any of us, yet, at the same time he was different, one of a kind. He was wild, funny, nearly as intelligent as his sister, and a charming rogue in the bargain. Whatever he did was always on a grander scale. He was the 'baddest' boy, flirting with danger. Skirting the edge, closer than any of the rest of us dared, yet he was never beyond redemption. At least not until the last.

"He had the charisma bad boys do. Women and men were drawn to him. Young, old and in between, they loved him." Jeb flexed his fingers, then closed them again into a fist. "I loved him. We were rivals and friends, and brothers. The sons of Apollo."

A wry smile jerked his lips in a grim twist. "Sounds ludicrous now, but then, when we lived to surf and play, the one thing that was as important was our brotherhood."

Mitch rumbled a wordless communion of empathy. The bond and trust of friendships were rare as he'd fought and clawed to survive the streets of the underbelly of New Orleans. But now he understood. The Watch had taught him. "You never saw anything?"

"To indicate what he really was?" Jeb looked down at the teakwood deck where shadows danced. "No." With an abrupt shrug that conveyed an absolute contempt he amended, "Nothing that concerned me as much as it should have. I was too busy raising hell to be clever."

"But there was something," Mitch persisted. There had to be. Something to explain this self-directed guilt.

"Maybe. If you call a look or the lack of reaction something. Nicole nearly drowned trying to do something he goaded her into, and it didn't upset him. I don't think he cared at all. After that, when he didn't know anyone was looking, his eyes would go flat, totally empty. Then he would laugh."

"As if he were putting you on. Fooling the world."

"He was. But we all thought we were. There were six of us, surfers first, thrill-seekers second. Anything else dead last. What we did was stupid, and, for the most part, innocuous. But I suppose it was inevitable there would be trouble."

"Drugs."

"By the grace of God, not my great common sense, I was involved only by association."

"The rest was by the grace of Simon," Mitch interjected.

The grace of Simon. Jeb hadn't heard it put quite like that before. But as rough and gruff and unrelenting as Simon could be, the analogy described, perfectly, an element common to most of the stories of the men of The Black Watch.

"Tony and I were already drifting apart," Jeb continued, and realized it was as much catharsis for himself as response to Mitch. "I can't give a specific reason. Yet, for the first time, I wasn't really sure of him. He was exonerated on the drug charge, but I wondered."

A shrug pulled his denim shirt close over the muscles of his shoulders and chest. A gold bracelet flashed on his wrist as he tugged a button free. "Maybe it was just happening. The natural progression of finally growing up. Who can say? Whatever the reason, graduation and Simon delivered the coup de grace."

Mitch chuckled, a sound at odds with the tone of their conversation. "I know the drill. He dragged you out of trouble by the scruff of your neck, damned you for a fool, slapped your wrist, then, before you knew it you were signed, sealed, recruited and committed."

"Something like that."

"Then The Watch became your life. No friends beyond its ranks. No lovers as important." Mitch waved an arm toward shore. "Just this."

He left Jeb to consider for himself the hours of work, the study, the subterfuge. A killer who had been a friend. An intriguing woman who might, or might not, be as innocent as she seemed.

Discovering there was no more to say, they sat in silence, each bound in his own thoughts of children and killers of children. Jeb knew rage seethed beneath Mitch's laconic comment. Someone had hurt a child—no, not someone, Tony had hurt a child. Another child.

Mitch would remember, and Tony wouldn't forget.

A trill of laughter rose from some faraway deck. The lantern gutted and died. Mitch stretched, yawned and rubbed his hand over his jaw. A gesture infinitely weary. Lurching to his feet, he yawned again. "I think I better get some shut-eye before I relieve the medicine man of his duty at the lady's house."

The medicine man, Matthew Sky. With his phenomenal night vision, it was without fail a foregone assumption he would take the night watch. Matthew never complained and, like Mitch, slept little.

"You gonna hang around?"

Not for the first time since he'd arrived bearing the news of Julie Brown, and battling his own sleeplessness, Jeb saw the toll the long hours had taken on his friend and colleague. Sliding back his chair, he stood, as well. "I'm heading back to the house."

"To get some sleep?"

"Maybe."

Mitch was too tired to argue. Three men, four if Bishop were included, made for a wretchedly small unit, spreading the duties heavily among them. It was Simon's call. Callison was smart, as intuitive as a cat. One man too many would flag his suspicions, and they could lose him completely.

They weren't the first of The Black Watch to work, virtually, around-the-clock. They wouldn't be the last.

At the steps leading below deck and to his bunk, Mitch paused. "Cap?"

"Yeah?"

"Have you ever regretted it? What Simon did to your life, I mean."

Jeb stroked his jaw, much as Mitch had. Two dedicated men, on the brink of exhaustion, facing truths. Perhaps for the first time. "Not often, and then not for long."

Mitch's head jerked in assent, a crooked smile lifted one corner of his mouth. "Neither have I, but don't tell the old fox. Wouldn't want him to be too cocky about it, would we?"

Jeb chuckled and waited. There was more.

"It wasn't insomnia that brought you to the *Gambler*."

No admission met the statement. No denial.

"There were things you needed to resolve about the little girl and Nicole."

Jeb's amusement vanished. "Some."

"Water's like fire, it soothes the brain and clears the mind."

"It does that."

"You know he killed her. Julie Brown, I mean."

"I know."

"Damn his black heart! A child!" Mitch's voice was strangled. "He just picked her at random, in the most unlikely place."

"A red herring." The words were mild, the look on Jeb's face was not. "He's laying a false trail, to confuse and confound whoever might be looking for him."

"Then you believe he's coming?"

"Now more than ever. The last contract, Jimmy Merino's son, shut the door to his usual contacts. Now both sides of the law want him. He has nowhere to turn but Nicole."

"What happens if the lady's righteous?"

Righteous? Innocent? Was she? "If it turns out that way, we'll move heaven and earth to keep her safe."

"If she's not?"

Jeb moved past Mitch, clapping a hand on his shoulder as he went. "You were going to get some shut-eye."

"Jeb." Not Cap, Jeb. A barometer of the depths of Mitch's disquiet. He waited until Jeb stepped on the dock to ask the question that concerned each of them in general, and Jeb specifically. "What happens if she knows what her brother is and means to help him?"

Jeb looked over the inlet, his gaze focused on a remote spot, facing what he'd known he must all along. When he turned back to Mitch his expression was stark. "Then I'll do whatever it takes."

I, not we. Jeb had assumed responsibility for the unthinkable.

The sound of his footsteps had faded from the boardwalk, and the roar of the roadster's engine was only a purr before Mitch made one last round to secure the sloop. Tonight marked a milestone for a man of conscience and honor. Jeb Tanner was senior agent, he would do what he must, no matter what it cost him. But it had been no secret from the first that he was deeply troubled by this assignment.

A troubled man made mistakes.

Tonight a last reservation had been put aside, and Mitch would rest easier for it.

Tonight Jeb Tanner had come to terms with himself.

* * *

"Good morning!"

At his greeting Nicole slowed her pace and stopped. She'd heard the steady thud of running footsteps behind her for some time and dismissed them. Joggers were rare on the beach at this early hour, but not unheard of. But Jeb was the last person she expected. "Jeb! What are you doing here?"

Bare, tanned chest heaving from his exertions, Jeb grinned and wiped a trickle of sweat from his forehead with the band at his wrist. "I live here. I'm your neighbor, six houses removed, remember?"

"Of course I remember. Surely you don't think I'd forget such an astounding coincidence. I just didn't expect you here, on the beach, at this hour." Jeb's visit to her house in Charleston had ended almost with the storm. In retrospect, she realized he spoke very little of himself beyond saying he'd done well in stocks, retired at thirty-seven, and lived on the island. He hadn't said why. "I can still hardly believe that after all these years we've both landed in this small corner of the world, on the same island."

"A happy coincidence, I hope."

"Certainly."

"Good, that's settled. Now, do you mind if I walk with you?"

"What about your run?"

"I've had enough, believe me. In fact I was singularly grateful when I recognized you and would have an excuse to stop."

Nicole laughed. "Is that what I am? An excuse?"

"No, Nicky, you're not an excuse." His gaze moved over her in lazy appreciation of the view just visible beneath her open shirt. Her skin was smooth and lustrous, the vibrant color of sun-warmed peaches. Her breasts were full, her body slender, and barely contained by an abbreviated shirt and twists of faded batik.

He'd seen more daring costumes on the beach. Bikinis and maillots cut down to the hips or up to the armpits. Almost.

And thongs! Lord, yes, thongs.

All of them in every fabric. Lycra and lamé, fishnet and sheers, practical or not, leaving little to the imagination. But none as tantalizing nor as intriguing as a suit that was modest in comparison. Stylish colors and sleek lines were no match for tattered scraps held together by tempting and tarnished U-rings.

No match at all, he discovered as he struggled to find the discipline to play the game he'd begun.

Forcing his attention from a body that would tempt a saint as well as the devil incarnate, his gaze wandered deliberately to safer ground. Touching first on hair that blazed like black fire in the sun as it tumbled over blacker brows, then lingering on sooty lashed eyes as green as a cool mountain lake. For a moment as he lost himself in them, he almost forgot to breathe, barely remembered to think.

Not safer ground. Not safe at all.

A mental shake reminded him where he was, and why. Nicole had to trust him, and more, if this was to work.

Lifting a hand to her face, he let his fingertips trail over the smooth slope of her cheek, skirted the corner of her mouth, toyed with the soft flesh of her lip.

"You're a beautiful woman." His voice was intimate, as smoky as his eyes. "An old friend I'd like to get to know again."

Her faltering smile vanished. Color flooded her face along with a flicker of something he couldn't quite interpret before she looked away.

"Hey!" He caught her chin in his fingers, lifting her face toward his as he bent nearer. "What's this?" His hand slipped to her cheek, cupping it, feeling the rush of heat, while the other stroked the line of her jaw. "I don't believe it, a blush! I didn't know women did that anymore."

"Don't." In a desperate move Nicole grasped his wrists and flung his hands from her. Her voice was grim, her words clipped. "Please don't touch me."

Her blush blanched to pallor. One as unexpected as the other, as extreme. Startled, he stepped back, hands raised, palms turned out in a pacific stance. "All right, I won't. But what's wrong, Nicky? What did I say? What did I do?"

"Don't pretend, and don't make fun. You never used to." She turned away, staring at the horizon where the sea blended into the sky. She couldn't look at him. She couldn't bear the mockery. Not from Jeb. Especially not from Jeb. "When everyone else considered it their favorite pastime, you never did."

"Make fun... Is that what you thought I was doing?" When she didn't answer, forgetting he'd said he wouldn't touch her, he caught her arm, turning her to him. "*Is* that what you thought I was doing?"

When she looked at him her gaze was steady and her eyes so intensely green from the effort they were nearly black. "Wasn't it?"

He saw the hurt and recalled the taunts, the cruel laughter aimed at a girl who was far too unsophisticated to realize they were prompted by envy. She was too young then, and too smart, and anyone with half a brain could see that one day she would be stunning. A pill too bitter for the intolerant, the less fortunate, and the covetous.

"No," he said in a gruff rumble. "Dear God, I wouldn't."

She was strong. She'd needed to be to withstand the taunts and to accomplish what she had. But buried deeply beneath that strength was an unexpected fragility. A surprising lack of conceit. He might be damned for a lying bastard before this was done. But he wouldn't pull the wings off a magnificent butterfly.

He moved a step closer, inordinately pleased that she hadn't pulled away from him again. His voice was low, soothing. "I was teasing, sweetheart. There is a difference."

She stared at him, searching his face, as if she were trying to decide if she should believe him. Jeb stood patiently, waiting for her decision, and wondered if no man had ever told her she was beautiful.

Nicole knew she was a fool for reacting as she had. Of course he was teasing. Her mind knew, but her heart wanted to believe every pretty word.

To silence the ache his bold stare and caressing touch had ignited in her she'd taken thoughtless refuge in bitterness. Accusing Jeb of cruelty she didn't believe.

"I'm sorry." She ran an agitated hand through her hair, the disarray only making her seem more vulnerable. "No one should know better than I that you wouldn't . . ."

"Laugh at you?" Jeb supplied the hateful words.

"Yes."

"I might laugh with you, sweetheart." He tapped her upturned nose and grinned again, relieved by the easy resolution of a difficult turn of events. "But I promise, never at you."

As he looked down at her, at the sweet, wobbly smile, Jeb wondered what might have been if he'd met her again in a different circumstance. If Tony Callison weren't her brother and Jeb Tanner could truly be the man he pretended.

It served no purpose to wonder, for circumstances could never be different, and what might have been was only a dream. There was no future for him here.

Not with this woman.

Nor with any woman.

With an unconscious regret for what he thought he never wanted, his hand skipped down her arm, fitting palm to palm, he laced his fingers through hers. When she left her hand in his, he drew a deep breath and held her tighter.

"Shall we start again, Nicky?" he asked. "Maybe this time we'll get it right."

Nicole nodded. She dared not trust her voice in the quicksilver shifting of his moods and hers, but with her hand in his, she was suddenly willing to try anything.

"Then would you do me the honor of a stroll through the sand, Ms. Callison?"

His grave and graceful bow should have been absurd for a man half dressed and on a sandy, sunlit beach. But it wasn't.

In the gallery, with casual clothing cloaking a body muscled and honed by his early years on the surf, he was virile and elegantly attractive. An accomplished, knowledgeable man of cold, utter calm. Once past the first delighted rush of recognition and friendship, the marvelous eyes that should have been the reflection of that man, had been shuttered, guarded, with little expression, offering no betrayal of his mood or thoughts.

She'd sensed, rather than seen, danger shimmering beneath the icy calm. Danger she hadn't understood. As he stood before her, holding her hand in his, bowing gallantly, she understood too well.

He was not cold here in the sun. He was not elegant, not merely attractive. As the light played over him, turning his sun-streaked hair to a tousled halo, and his skin to burnished gold, he was too vivid, too alive to be merely anything.

Running shorts, wet from the sweat of exertion and clinging, left little doubt he was undeniably, powerfully masculine. A rogue's grin tugging at his mouth, and a glint in his eyes, he was pure animal magnetism. And in his gray gaze keeping hers, locked deeply within dark-rimmed irises, she discovered the primal man.

A man of fire and ice. A man of raw passions and ruthless anger, of fear and love and secret hurt. The man she'd loved all her life. Untamed, intriguing and infinitely hazardous to her good sense. There lay the danger.

"Shall we walk, Nicky? Shall we pretend this is Eden, and ours are the only footsteps that have ever crossed the sand?"

As he spoke he bent nearer, his breath brushing her cheek. The heated scent of him rose to her, filling her lungs with the fragrance of soap and sweat and man.

Danger. Her mind cried it, her heart didn't listen.

Nicole knew she should back away. Perhaps run away. She wasn't ready for the tenderness, nor the warmth. There was too much she had to resolve, to put into perspective. Too much she had to understand about herself, and what she might still feel for Jeb.

She should have backed away. Should have run. Instead she heard herself saying, "There's nothing I'd like better than to walk with you and pretend there's no one here but us."

An hour later, after they'd chased scrabbling crabs to their high-water lairs, stalked drowsing gulls and raced with the sandpipers like mischievous children, Nicole's misgivings were forgotten.

Until Jeb stopped scuffing sand dollars from their bur-
rows at the water's edge, to watch her.

Feeling his stare, Nicole looked up from the array of shells
she'd collected in her shirt. Thinking he was amused by the
fine layer of sand covering her nose, with a quirk of her lips
and a huffing breath she blew it away.

And still he stared and smiled.

Just for a while, she tried to stare him down, but he was
impervious. His eyes were on her, but his mind seemed to see
into her. She tried to ignore him, going about the business
of lining sand dollars to dry in the sand. And still his rivet-
ing stare followed her. Nettled by the scorching intensity, she
bolted to her feet, spilling shirt and spiny disks helter-skelter
on the sand.

"What?" she demanded, feet planted, hands on narrow
hips. "What on earth fascinates you so much?"

"You do," he said almost absently. "Only you, my love."

"Of course I do. I'm an old friend, remember?" She
made the saucy remark with a brash bravado, ignoring the
sudden trip-hammer pace of her heart. Then in spite of
every effort to the contrary, she asked, "Why, Jeb?"

"I'm damned if I know." He spoke scarcely above the
sound of the surf. "I suppose it could be that it's almost too
easy to believe we're the only people who've ever walked this
shore. One man, one woman in a sandy Eden."

Nicole wanted to say something. Another bantering reply, a facetious observation, but her tongue wouldn't co-
operate.

He didn't seem to notice. "It could be that wee bit of a
swimsuit you're wearing. Little strips of cloth that are
nothing more than color on skin do strange things to a
man's blood pressure."

"My suit?" Nicole looked down at the ancient bikini.
When she'd taken her shirt off to gather up the sand dollars he'd found, she hadn't given it a thought. In fact, she'd
forgotten the suit was faded and so thin...

"Oh no!" So thin every contour of her breasts and nip-
ples showed as clearly as if she were naked.

"Oh, yes." Jeb slanted her a grin.

"Oh, Lord, you must think..."

"I haven't been thinking anything, except how I could persuade you to take the rest of the day off from work."

"Work? The rest of the day?"

"It is Monday, isn't it? You did plan to open the gallery."

"Oh, no." She raised her face skyward, finding the fully risen sun. "What time is it?"

"Ten minutes past the time you should have left the island. *If* you were going to open the gallery."

"There's no 'if' to it. I have an appointment with the old biddy today."

"The old biddy?"

"Mrs. Atherton,"

"Of course, Mrs. Atherton." He had no idea who Mrs. Atherton was.

"She's a pain in the tush and a snob, but she does spend a lot of money with us." Nicole shaded her eyes and squinted at the sun again, judging her chances of making the appointment. "How late did you say it was?"

"A minute later than when you asked before."

"Eleven minutes, I can do that." Then she was running down the beach, like a dark-haired child racing with the wind.

"Nicole!" When she didn't answer, he called again. "Nicole! What are you going to do?"

She whirled about in the sand, her hair flying, her breasts nearly spilling from the suit as it threatened to slide into ignominy. "I'm going to make up eleven minutes."

"You can't."

"Yes I can. Just pray that Charlie's not on duty today."

"Charlie? Who's Charlie?"

"The patrolman who loves to play coyote and roadrunner with me." The last was tossed over her shoulder as she settled into a ground-eating jog.

"Wait," Jeb called as he waded out of the water. Scooping up her shirt, he watched as she turned left and raced up a bank of stairs. She disappeared over a dune as he finished what he'd meant to say. "You forgot your shirt."

* * *

"I should have known," Nicole muttered as she tossed her jacket aside. Kicking off her shoes, she sank into a chaise, poured a glass of wine and propped her aching feet, one over the other. With her eyes closed, she raised the tulip-shaped goblet to her forehead, soothing lines of repressed anger with its delicate bowl.

Without opening her eyes, she listened to the surf wash over the shore as she sipped the wine. She'd poured a dark, velvety cabernet, not her usual Riesling or Grenache. For tonight she'd wanted something rich and bold with a kick. As she'd wanted to kick Mrs. Atherton, straight out of the gallery.

"Hypocrite," she declared and sipped again. "There ought to be a law."

Settling farther into the chaise lounge, she considered dinner, and dismissed it. It was too late, and she was far too comfortable to bother. After today she deserved a quiet, comfortable evening.

She'd just drained her second glass and was succumbing to a delicious little haze when the bell at the front door rang. The temptation to ignore it was strong, and she was still considering it when the bell rang twice more in quick succession.

"I should have known." She struggled from the chaise. "A perfect ending to a perfect day."

Not bothering to find her shoes, she padded to the door, the crinkled fabric of her skirt brushing over her bare feet. Normally she would have checked to see who was calling. Thanks to an empty stomach and two glasses of wine drunk faster than usual, she didn't trouble herself with the effort.

The door banged against the wall as she flung it open with obvious irritation. "Yes?" she hissed then blinked. "Jeb?"

"Yep." He lounged against the wall, laughing down at her. Her shirt dangled from a crooked finger. "Always turning up, like the proverbial penny."

"What penny?" The gaze she turned to his was vague and slightly unfocused.

"Uh-oh." He drew away from the wall, and at his full height towered over her. "Bad day?"

"You could say that, considering the way that it started."

"Funny, I sorta liked the way it started."

"You're making fun." She squinted up at him. "Are you making fun? You promised you wouldn't. Never, never make fun. Fun hurts."

Jeb shook his head and eased the glass from her fingers only an instant before it would have slipped from her loose grasp. Holding it up to the light spilling through the door, he saw the dark red color of the drop that was left. "How many of these have you had?"

"Two." She waved three fingers in his face. "Only two."

"Oh dear." Jeb smothered a smile and wondered if she couldn't count, or had the least tolerance for wine of anyone he'd ever seen.

"Oh dear, is exactly right. This has been an 'oh dear' sort of day, all day long." Her skirt dipped and swayed, and the square cut neck of her camisole dipped with it, revealing a tantalizing bit of femininity as she leaned against the door.

"It has, has it?" He wouldn't think of the camisole, soft and supple, provocative in its very simplicity, and leaving little doubt her breasts were naked beneath it.

"In... innnndubitably."

"Then why don't we fix it?" Stepping forward, he swept her into his arms, and was surprised to discover how well she fit next to his heart. How good she felt in his embrace.

"What...?" Woozy from the swiftness of his move, she clung to him, her arms wrapped tightly about his neck.

"Shh," Jeb murmured against her hair. "Just relax. This won't hurt a bit. I promise."

"Jeb?"

"None other."

With a step unhampered by the slight addition of her weight, he crossed to the deck and settled with her into the chaise. A glance at her demure little jacket tossed carelessly aside, and her shoes tumbled heel over toe as if a tottering child had abandoned them, told a story of irritation and frustration. The bottle of wine with so little taken from it proved a suspicion that she'd eaten little if anything all day. Explaining how two glasses of wine came to be verified so emphatically with three fingers.

"Knocked you on your pretty little tush didn't it, sweetheart?" Her shirt and his excuse, lay crumpled and forgotten by the door.

"Hmm?" She moved restlessly against him, her cheek scrubbing his chest.

"Shh." He considered dinner, then decided food was not what she needed. Drawing her close, he stroked her hair, breathing in her perfume as it blended with the fresh sea air. A seductive combination as intoxicating as the wine. For his own sanity he didn't want to think of her perfume, any more than he wanted to think of the camisole, or her body curled into his. But he wasn't destined to succeed in that, and as he eased her tensions his own escalated. With an uneven note in his voice he murmured, "Why don't you tell me about your day."

"My day was terrible." Each word was carefully spaced.

"So you said."

"It started with you."

"That was terrible?"

"Yes. No. I don't know."

"Maybe we'd better leave that part out for now. What came next?"

"Charlie coyote came next."

"Ah-ha! He caught the roadrunner. How fast?"

"Just eighty-five miles an hour."

"Just! That's not running, honey, it's flying low. What next?"

"Mrs. Atherton."

"The old biddy."

"In the flesh. She wants Ashley's paintings. She hates him and calls him the village idiot, and *that* woman's child. Whoever *that* woman is. Ashley's paintings aren't for sale. If they were, I wouldn't sell them to someone who called him an idiot."

"Good for you."

"You wouldn't say that if you knew how close I came to spitting in her eye and banning her from the gallery forever."

"Our little cygnet grew into a magnificent swan with a

tiger's heart," Jeb whispered against her temple. "Tony would be proud of you."

His first mention of her brother. He waited for her reaction.

"Ha!" She clutched at his shirt and curled closer into him. Her hand trembled. "He wouldn't care at all."

Jeb held her, daring no more as she struggled with something he didn't understand. It was a long while before her ragged breaths slowed to a drowsy rhythm and when he rose from the chaise, she clung to him, muttering sleepily into his throat. It was a simple matter to find her bedroom. But not so simple to listen to his head and not his body as he stripped away her skirt and discovered the camisole was a chemise. A single garment intended to serve the utilitarian purpose of both lingerie and blouse.

"Utilitarian! Like hell!" he growled on a strangled breath. It was madness dressed up in lace, lying in wait for an unsuspecting male.

He was suddenly and, he knew, unfairly angry with her for what he felt, for what she made him feel. But anger became his temporary ally. When he left her sleeping like a trusting child with the duvet tucked chastely beneath her chin, beyond the intimate glimpse, he knew little more about Nicole Callison. And because of it, a damnable lot about himself.

He wanted her. He might curse himself for a fool and an idiot, but it changed nothing.

Guilty, or innocent, he wanted her.

Four

The sun was past its meridian as Jeb slipped the roadster into a narrow slot in the unpaved lot. Shadows pooled in elongated circles about live oaks and blooming crape myrtles. In this late afternoon hour, the hottest part of the day, the purposeful pedestrian would find no relief in them from the sultry heat rising from the walks of Charleston.

A wise man would have gone to ground, seeking out the cool, or creating his own with a long, cold drink. A worried man would do exactly as Jeb, seeking out the cause of his worry.

As he stepped into the galley, his first impression was of an island of cool serenity in the midst of the sweltering heat outside. A quiet day winding down to a quieter end. In the space of a thought, the illusion was shattered by the caustic demand of the lone customer.

"You might as well sell, Nicole. I intend to have the paintings, sooner or later." Haughty flint in the commanding voice was not softened by a cultured drawl. "Sooner would be much easier, my dear, for all of us."

"The paintings aren't for sale, Mrs. Atherton." Nicole was calm, only the set of her shoulders betrayed annoyance.

"Of course they are." The regal woman with an unyieldingly straight back and perfectly groomed silver hair gestured with the arrogance of royalty. Her lust focused on a group of paintings hanging in an obvious place of honor. "Why else would you display them at the sale?"

"They were only lent to us. I can't sell what isn't mine." Nicole dealt with peremptory arrogance with unshakable composure.

"You're being ridiculous, Nicole." The woman was taller, larger, and by the sheer power of her size and her position in the city, she meant to intimidate the younger, smaller upstart.

Jeb's initial inclination was to step in, but something in the look of Nicole held him back. Settling back against a column, he crossed his arms over his chest and observed, discovering he needn't have worried.

"I'm not being ridiculous, and I'm not being stubborn." Nicole was undaunted, her pleasant attitude unchanged. "I'm keeping a promise."

"To whom?"

"To Ashley, Mrs. Atherton," Annabelle interjected from her desk, her black eyes burning into the woman like lasers.

"No one asked you, Annabelle." Mrs. Atherton sent her a scathing look meant to remind an underling of her place.

"Perhaps you didn't ask Annabelle, but what she says is true. My agreement and my promise to Ashley in return for the privilege of displaying his paintings was that they wouldn't be sold."

"The man's an idiot. He wouldn't know if you sold one, or two or the whole lot of them. A promise to Ashley means no more than a promise to a stray dog."

"Ashley is *not* a stray, Mrs. Atherton." Twin wings of color swept across Nicole's cheeks as her face paled. The shaking of her hand was stilled by a convulsive tightening of her fingers over a gold clad fountain pen.

The grande dame of Charleston didn't seem to notice, but Jeb did, as the foolish woman waded deeper into the fray. "He lives on the street, Nicole, that's virtually the same."

"He might wander the streets, but he doesn't live on them. He has a house, not a mansion like yours, but functional. And he has a job."

"Shining shoes in a hotel?"

"It's honest work that meets his needs. And—" warning that there was more, was given by only the slightest force in Nicole's voice " —just because he isn't like you, or anyone else in Charleston, doesn't mean he's an idiot. But if he were, why would you include the work of an idiot you so despise in your hallowed collection?"

"Nicole!" The pinched, elderly face grew even more autocratic. "You needn't be rude."

"You're right," Nicole agreed. "It's the last thing I need." Crossing to Annabelle's desk, she laid the pen on a colorful blotter. Her breasts rose in a long, deep breath before she turned back to her obstinate customer. "Ashley's paintings are not for sale, Mrs. Atherton, that precludes the need for more discussion. Now, if you will excuse me, we close in ten minutes and I have things to do."

"I will not excuse you, Nicole, I—"

"Nicky, darling," Jeb said softly as he pushed away from the column and moved toward the desk. He'd heard enough, and more. He was tired of the woman's arrogance, and amazed she didn't see the stony look in eyes as cold as green ice. "Have you forgotten?"

"Forgotten?" Nicole turned to him, a flash of surprise on her face. Engrossed as she'd been with her contest of will with Mrs. Atherton, she had no idea he had come to the gallery and even less what she might have forgotten. "I'm sorry, I don't..."

"Ahh, sweetheart." He folded his palms about her cheeks. As surprise ascended to shock, he brushed her mouth with his, lightly, but with a lingering completeness. With unmistakable reluctance he moved away, accusing tenderly, "You forgot our date."

"Our date?" Nicole touched her lips with an unsteady hand. Amid the sudden tumult of every nerve, she realized she sounded like a parrot, but at just this particular moment, she couldn't quite get her jangled thoughts in order. "What date?"

"Ohmigosh!" Annabelle slapped her forehead with an open hand. "I'm the one who forgot, Jeb. *I* forgot to tell Nicole you called. She has no idea you've planned a romantic dinner just for the two of you." Rising from her desk, like a minuscule queen of the Amazons, she crossed to Mrs. Atherton. Taking her arm firmly, she led the speechless woman to the door. "I'm sure you understand that we need to close a tad early today."

"No, I don't." Unaccustomed to such cavalier treatment, the self-acclaimed savant of the arts struggled to remove her arm from Annabelle's grasp, but discovered the pudgy hand gripped like a vice.

"Of course you don't mind." Annabelle cut short her protest. "I'm sure you realize as well as I how impatient young lovers can be."

"Young lovers?" The covert struggle ceased, avid eyes stared at Nicole and Jeb over Annabelle's shoulder.

"Yes, indeedy, it's wonderful, isn't it?" The gallery door was open. The pressure of Annabelle's hand had to be bruising as she stepped into the street with Mrs. Atherton. "*Do* come to see us again, soon. Surely by then we'll have something you'll like as well as Ashley's paintings."

One step back, a hearty shove of the door and the newest Amazon turned to face them. "There now." She dusted her hands on her skirt as if the touch of Mrs. Atherton left them soiled. "As of this minute, we are officially closed."

"Annabelle," Nicole managed to utter, "do you know what you just did?"

"Indeed, I do. Exactly what I've always wanted to do—throw the old battle-ax out."

"Bravo!" Jeb clapped his hands.

"And you!" Nicole rounded on him. "Do you know what *you've* just done?"

"Indeed, I do." Jeb rested one hip on the edge of Annabelle's desk as he brushed a wisp of ebony from Nicole's temple. "I just saved the old battle-ax's life. I don't believe she realized how close you were to losing your temper."

"I might get angry, but I don't lose my temper," Nicole said through clenched teeth.

"No, I'm sure you don't. It isn't allowed, is it? That's why you have nights like last night, when you're wound so tight."

"I wasn't wound tight." She dodged away from him.

Jeb chuckled. "No, I don't suppose you were." Undeterred by her abrupt move, he stroked her hair. A not so subtle reminder that he'd done the same in the moonlight on a deck overlooking the sea. "Just tight."

Nicole caught his wrist, her fingers closing like handcuffs over the tanned flesh. "I was not tight then, I'm not angry now."

"You're not angry." Jeb agreed conversationally.

"No, I'm not angry."

"Hey! Who's arguing?" Her hands still circled his wrists, he left them there. "Then it's settled, you're going to dinner with me."

Nicole released her grasp as if his touch burned and backed away. "I will not go to dinner with you."

"Then you're angry with me."

"I am not."

Jeb grinned, propped one foot over the other, and crossed his arms over his chest. "Then, sweetheart, tell me why."

"Because."

"Because, why?"

"Because I have work to do."

"Name it."

"I have to close the gallery."

"Annabelle just did that."

"I certainly did," Annabelle murmured from her vantage point by the door.

"Anything else, Nicky?" Jeb asked.

"There are new paintings to catalog."

"I can do that," Annabelle piped in.

"I have some packages to ready for shipping."

"That, too."

"Annabelle." Nicole turned to her assistant. "You need to get home to your husband. He must be disturbed with the long hours we've been working."

"No, I don't, Harry isn't home. That's why I don't mind hanging out here—it gets lonesome in that rambling old house without my hot-blooded stallion around."

"Give it up, Nicky. You're surrounded, and the cavalry isn't coming." Jeb straightened to his full height, standing just a couple of inches under a foot taller than her five feet, two. "You avoided me this morning by skipping your walk on the beach. The evening's another matter.

"Unless, you want to break one of your own cardinal rules, and lose your temper." He touched her chin, tracing the small indentation that was not quite a cleft. "Do you want to be angry with me? Do you blame me for last night?" He lifted her face to his. "Would you feel better if we pretended it never happened?"

Annabelle made a restless move, her curiosity building to volcanic proportions. A warning glance from Jeb quieted her.

Nicole wasn't aware of the restlessness or the warning. She didn't look away from Jeb, or move from the lazy, mesmerizing caress. He was right, she had avoided the beach and another chance encounter. When she'd woken with the first chirping of the birds, she was disoriented and had no memory of retiring the night before. When a headache struck, the magnitude of which only red wine could cause, she was confused. When she discovered she was still dressed in her chemise, she remembered Jeb.

Jeb. Lounging by her door in the moonlight. Catching her glass, then scooping her up, as well. Soothing her, teasing her, listening to the debacle that had been her day.

Jeb. His lips in her hair. The beat of his heart against her own. His hands on her as he stripped off her skirt. His angry, half-whispered curse as he found what she wore beneath.

Jeb. His soft kiss on her forehead. His quiet wish for a restful sleep.

Jeb. Awakening every dream she'd ever dreamed. Dreams that had lain silent, but never died.

Jeb. Always Jeb. Her heart would never be free of him. And she was a fool.

Since then, her day and her mood had vacillated to the extreme, the single constant had been self-contempt and humiliation. She almost welcomed a second day of Mrs. Atherton's demands. At least it was something to think about other than Jeb and her own stupidity.

Now there was nothing to do but face it and brazen it out if she must. "I don't suppose there's any need in lying. I did avoid you this morning—I thought you would prefer it that way. I...uh...wasn't exactly myself. I hope you know that. I don't usually do that sort of thing and to inflict myself upon you was unforgivable. We were friends in the past, but, if we're honest, we have to admit we're almost strangers now."

Annabelle gasped and made an odd choking sound.

Jeb heard, knew exactly the connotation she'd given Nicole's rambling monologue, and couldn't resist the temptation to strike a flame to smoldering suspicion. "We aren't strangers, my love." He whispered softly, but not too softly. "We could never be after last night."

"I thought you would be disappointed in me."

"The only thing that disappoints me, is that you've refused to have dinner with me." He took her hands in both of his. "Would it be so awful to spend another evening with me? This time I promise I won't put you to bed."

Nicole succumbed to laughter and to him. He was teasing her, and the anger she'd heard last night was gone. "All right, it's a deal. But this time I promise, you won't need to put me to bed."

"Deal." He kissed the tender flesh of one wrist and backed away. "I'll browse while you freshen up."

Nicole hurried to a set of doors that led to a small lounge and bathroom. Annabelle didn't have to be a clairvoyant to interpret one last tarrying look. Her cool, collected boss wasn't so cool and collected and wasn't sure at all what she was getting herself into.

Jeb moved through the gallery, pausing before this painting and that. Patting the head of a bronze retriever and the nose of a perky chipmunk. When he drew near the wolf's head, Annabelle was waiting as he knew she would be. As Mrs. Atherton said, sooner or later.

"Ahh, Annabelle." He smiled down at her. "I imagine you have some questions for me."

"You bet I do." She jerked her head toward the wolf, a magnificent rendering that captured danger and spirit without taming either. "Judging from this little conversation, it sounds as if you might be trying to live up to your reincarnation here."

"In other words, you think I'm trifling with your boss lady."

"Are you? Did you?" Blunt question, brooking nothing but truth. Jeb would give her that, in part. He wondered what she would think of the whole of it.

"If by trifling, you mean did I sleep with Nicole last night. The answer is no, Annabelle."

"But she said—"

"She said I put her to bed. And I did. Alone."

The dark, Gypsy mane swayed about plump shoulders as a skeptical chin jutted at him. "Suppose you explain how that came about."

"All right." Jeb traced the proud profile of the wolf, then dropped his hand away. "Not that it's any of your business."

"Nicole, and anyone who might hurt her, is my business."

"Not that it's any of your business," Jeb repeated mildly, "but I'll tell you."

"So tell." Annabelle's tiny feet were planted firmly before him. With her arms folded over her considerable bosom, she was the embodiment of the immovable object. "I'm waiting."

"It's simple. She'd had a rough day, little or nothing to eat. Fatigue, frustration, hunger and two quick glasses of red wine combined for an unexpected circumstance. When I arrived at her door, she was, shall we say, a bit unsteady on her feet."

"Nicole never drinks too much."

"I can't and won't dispute that. It wouldn't have been too much then, if someone had seen to it she hadn't neglected to eat."

"You mean me."

"No, Annabelle, at least not just you. Nicole herself should have seen to it."

"She was distracted, and then Mrs. Atherton came in spewing her ugliness." She was quicker to defend Nicole than herself.

"Did Nicky say what was bothering her?"

"Nicole, Nicky as you call her, doesn't talk about her problems. She's a good listener if you need one, but she doesn't expect the same in return." Black eyes narrowed as a thought occurred. "She's never mentioned any family, or you. I knew she was from California, because I'm good with accents, remember. We do talk about it and her schooling. Not a pleasant experience from the little I can gather. But nothing else."

"Does she mention her brother?"

"Only to say you were her brother's friend. And that was only after I grilled her unmercifully the day you first came to the gallery."

Jeb wanted to hear more, but he dared not raise this astute woman's mistrust any more. "She's done well here." A gesture encompassed the gallery, Charleston, the island. "How did it all happen?"

"It happened because she's a smart, savvy lady. Because she worked like a slave, practically nonstop from the first."

"What was the first? Help me understand, Annabelle." He could have been an interested old friend, a hopeful lover. His first judgment of her career was of a wasted mind, but as he recognized her instinctive knowledge and understanding of the world of art, he viewed her choice in a new perspective.

Annabelle inclined her head, as if she understood his burning need to know. "She began on a small scale, dealing with estate sales, taking stock on consignment. She was so young people were leery at first. But she was honest to a fault, and her knowledge of art was so incredible, so far reaching, it wasn't long before word spread. One dowager was so pleased with her, and with the collection Nicole helped her acquire, she appointed herself Nicole's patron. When she died, to Nicole's complete bewilderment, she bequeathed her this building, a goodly portion of her art and the single on Jessamine Street.''

"How long have you worked for her?"

"From the first. With the exception of some packers called in before and after a sale or auction, there is only one other employee. Ravenel Rollins, a retired professor, who knows nearly as much about the business as Nicole.''

"That means you have known her, how long?"

"Seven years.''

"In all that time, Nicole has never mentioned her family?" He was doubling back, asking the same question more than once, in different contexts. An old and tried interrogator's trick.

"Never." Annabelle was adamant and unwavering.

"Tell me of the men in her life."

Shoulders lifting in an expression of uncertainty, her arms spread for emphasis, Annabelle said, "Who knows? If there has ever been anyone, he was only a passing fancy. If one has ever been more than that, she kept him a dark secret. She kept you secret."

"There was nothing to keep secret, Annabelle. Fifteen years ago, she was fifteen, I was twenty-two. For a while we were friends, nothing more."

"You're certain?"

Jeb inclined his head once, sharply. "Certain."

A dark, hot gaze swept over him, the lids nearly slitted. "Then, Jeb Tanner, I think you must be a fool."

"You two are certainly deep in serious conversation. Private? Or can anyone join in?"

Jeb had been so intent on his questions and the responses they elicited, he hadn't heard Nicole until she spoke. He turned now, superimposing a smile over the frown Annabelle's last remark had drawn from him. In an instant everything was forgotten.

Nicole had taken the time to freshen the makeup that was a mere dusting of color over her even features. Only the jacket she'd worn had been changed for another. He wouldn't have believed the addition of a single garment could make such a startling transformation.

The first was loose, unconstructed, with a collar buttoned about her neck. The discarded pale blue-green silk blended with, but was not a match to the darker, full skirt. The fitted jacket that replaced it was the same, rich turquoise, completing a charming suit. From the sliver of black lace visible between its classical lapels, he knew beyond any doubt the only garment she wore beneath it was a chemise.

Images of her strong and supple young body wrapped in scant gossamer and moonlight streaming through her bedroom window assailed him. The vagaries of memory turned silk to lace, and turquoise to sultry black. He knew before he looked that her eyes would no longer be blue.

"You're stunning." He meant it literally. Looking at her dazed him. She was a vision in wonderful hues that turned her dusky skin tawny, and her ever changeable eyes to sultry green.

"Flattery, sir?" She slipped her arm through his.

Jeb didn't answer. He was struck again by her complete lack of conceit.

"Of course it's flattery, of the best kind. The truth," Annabelle groused. With a wave and a wiggle of her fingers she urged them to the door. "You two have better things to do than hang out here. Just remember, tomorrow I expect a play-by-play report."

"One question before we go," Nicole insisted.

"For whom?" Jeb asked.

"Both of you."

"Shoot," Annabelle chimed in.

Nicole looked from one to the other. "There was no telephone call, was there?"

Jeb glanced at Annabelle, and she at him.

"Never mind," Nicole said thoughtfully. "The two of you made this whole fiasco up as you went along."

"You needed to eat," Jeb offered as his alibi. "You aren't big enough to afford skipping meals two consecutive days."

"Anything to get Mrs. Atherton out of your hair." Annabelle looked no less contrite than Jeb.

"In other words, you've appointed yourselves my guardian angels, whether I like it or not." Nicole's tone was stern.

"Yes," a masculine and a gruff feminine voice declared in unison.

The scowl on Nicole's face faded. A radiant smile replaced it. "Thank you," she said. "For caring."

Nicole was still smiling as she walked arm in arm with Jeb down the street.

"Be careful, boss lady," Annabelle mused as she watched them out of sight. "There's a wolf at your door, a handsome, dangerous wolf."

Where there had been sun, now there was moonlight. The city streets were quiet, subdued in the lazy gentility that seemed to descend with the night.

After dinner, Jeb strolled with Nicole over uneven brick walks, past walled gardens with their ornate gates and lush foliage peeking from them. Old houses displaying curious earthquake bolts, cul-de-sacs with cloistered shops, and horse-drawn carriages with drivers dressed in top hat and tails, creating an aura of the past that enchanted and enfolded them.

As they walked, Jeb could visualize Charleston as early travelers had seen it. Wooded shores, deep bays, accessible harbors. Church spires towering over Adamesque and Georgian mansions, singles with graceful porches and piazzas. He understood why they'd stayed, why Nicole had chosen the city and the island for her homes.

Nicole equated his silence with her own wonder at the enduring memory of a gentler life-style. "You can almost see them, can't you?"

"The people of old Charleston?"

Nicole looked into the facade of one of the larger singles as they passed it. "Imagine it. Supper would be over by this hour. They've dined on vegetables brought down the rivers from plantation gardens, oranges from Florida, pineapple from Cuba, the finest wines of France, and coffee from South America. After the table is cleared the gentlemen tarry in the dining room over port or brandy, the ladies retire to the drawing room for tea."

"An idyllic time, if one didn't look too closely." Jeb hadn't intended the cynical edge in his comment. The evening had gone too well to blunder now. "Sorry." He shrugged. "Didn't mean to spoil your mood."

"You haven't. The system wasn't really so pretty. But warts and all, the golden era of the seventeenth and eighteenth centuries contributed in making Charles Towne Colony the city it is today."

"With modern warts."

"Yes." She burst out laughing and took his arm as they crossed the street to Waterfront Park. "With modern warts."

The park was unexpectedly deserted and they wandered alone through ancient magnolias and sword-leafed palmettos. At a railing overlooking the harbor, Nicole stopped, leaning her elbows on the iron. "I love this place."

"Do you come here often?"

"Only when dashing gentlemen offer dinner at Saracen."

"Have there been many gentlemen, Nicole?"

"Alas, no." She turned her back to the harbor, leaning again against the iron rail.

"Why not?" It was beyond conception that the gallants of Charleston wouldn't pursue her. If there hadn't been men in her life, it wouldn't be of their choosing.

"At first, I think it was that I was too busy. Getting established in Charleston wasn't easy. Later..." She lifted a shoulder in an eloquent expression of her loss for words. "I suppose it was the gallery then."

"Or that you lacked the inclination?" Jeb suggested.

"Perhaps." She pushed away from the fence to wander the path again.

The subject was closed, and Jeb needed to know why. He would have his answer, but not tonight. He wouldn't push. His subtle interrogation over dinner beneath the towering arched windows of the Saracen had been enough. He was content to know that Nicole's version of her early days in Charleston matched her assistant's.

A third source wouldn't be overlooked, Mitch or Matthew, not Jeb, must speak with Mrs. Atherton. Tomorrow, while she was still angry and would put no sugar coating on what she knew.

Nicole moved deeper into the shadows. Away from the light, into darkness that would be her shield. Jeb mustn't see by any telltale look she couldn't hide that it was more than lack of inclination that destroyed any budding liaisons before they began. Far more.

The sound of water splashing from a fountain faded, and for a while they walked side by side, neither speaking. Each lost in thoughts of guilt.

A twig cracked. A low sweeping tree limb rustled where there was no wind. The park was suddenly still.

Jeb caught her arm, his grip hard, commanding. A finger to his lips stopped her startled protest. He drew her closer, his body as much shield as the darkness. Not moving, not daring a breath, he listened.

Nothing. No buzzing insects, no flutter of birds' wings, no furtive scurrying of tiny night creatures.

Too quiet.

Too still.

Something, or someone, had disturbed the natural order of the night.

Jeb's stare probed the shadows, distinguishing small shrubs and plants, park benches and low signs. In the concealing cover of a drooping magnolia, there was only utter blackness.

"What?" Nicole breathed the question as she clutched the open throat of his shirt.

Jeb shook his head. His breath ruffled her hair as he leaned closer. "I'm not sure."

"Then how..."

"Shh." He stopped her with a palm over her mouth. "Listen," he said quietly as he moved his hand away. "What do you hear?"

Head tilted in an air of concentration, she did as he ordered. "Nothing," she said at last. "I don't hear anything. The park is quiet." With a sudden gasp she raised a stricken gaze to his. "Too quiet."

Jeb's hold on her tensed, his head turned right, then left, then ever so slowly, right again. "Almost."

Nicole didn't know if he meant almost too quiet, or that he'd almost discovered the source of the intrusion. Before she could ask, he was turning her into his embrace, holding her so close her breasts were crushed against his chest.

"Kiss me," he muttered. A command not an invitation.

"What?" Nicole jerked her face toward his. "Why—"

"Shut up and do as I say." Gray eyes as passionless and cold as ash in the moonlight bored into hers. "Put your arms around my neck and kiss me."

When she hesitated, a low growl rose from the depths of his chest. "Now, dammit."

She would have refused. In sheer perversity in the face of masculine audacity, she would have told him in less than ladylike terms what he could do with himself. And kissing wasn't one of them. Maybe it was the park, a stillness too still, a silence too silent. Maybe it was the urgency she heard beneath the arrogant command that had her sliding her hands over his chest to his shoulders, then his nape. Drawing him down as she rose on tiptoe, her mouth played over his. A chaste kiss, a taste, given with trembling lips that nearly betrayed her.

As she sank back to the pavement, she was visibly shaking. Her eyes were wide and luminous, rivaling the moon. But Jeb had no time to admire or to comfort.

"Again," he commanded in a guttural hiss. "This time as if you mean it."

"Jeb." Nicole put a staying hand on his chest, needing room to think. To breathe.

"Now!" His fingers curled around her shoulders, driving into them, lifting her to him. "Like this," he muttered, and something ignited the cold ashes of his gaze as his mouth closed over hers.

His kiss was harsh, the fierceness of his grip an omen of bruises tomorrow. Ten of them, one for each punishing fingertip. Their ache was a memory unrelieved even as his hands slipped to her hair, cupping her head in his palms, drawing her closer still. The thrust of his body against hers was hard, as fierce as his touch.

His hands tugged back her head, his mouth scorched the flesh of her throat as it ranged over it. A sound, a sigh or cry, shuddered through him and he drew her closer, closer, his body a brand.

"Like this," he breathed against her skin as he felt her yield. His kiss was punishment, his mouth still harsh, demanding she yield more and yet more.

Nicole's head was spinning, her heart racing. No man had held her as Jeb was holding her. None had provoked her or angered her as he, demanding what could very nearly destroy her. Allowing no refusal.

Then there would be none.

"No." She muttered her anger against his lips. Her fingers tangled in his hair, her nails furrowing his scalp. "Like this."

Her mouth opened beneath his, her teeth catching the tender curve of his bottom lip. Jeb groaned, but not in pain, and his tongue teased over hers. Anger vanished in the avalanche of more primal needs and Nicole was spinning, falling into a world she'd never known. He tasted of brandy and desperation, and she never wanted it to stop. Never wanted to let him go.

Yet even as she clung to him, he was stepping back, catching her wrists in a gentler grasp, dragging them down his body. She could feel the force of his heartbeat, and the ragged rise of his chest as he struggled for calm.

"Yes," he said softly. "Like that." Drawing her to his side, he draped an arm about her shoulders. "Put your arms around my waist. Now, lean your head on my shoulders. We're going to walk very carefully into the darkness. Two desperate lovers seeking a secret place to make the love they feel."

Nicole tensed and would have pulled away, but he kept her close. "Easy. You've played your part, don't lose it now." In a whispery singsong, he encouraged her, praised her, until the darkness of a gigantic magnolia swallowed them. "Great. You're doing great."

Releasing her he stripped off the jacket he'd worn to satisfy whatever dress codes the Saracen might impose. Spreading it on the ground, he took her hand and drew her down with him.

Nicole had gone beyond objection, a part of her knew dimly he wouldn't listen. When he kissed her again, she responded. Playing her role, she insisted, even as he leant her back, pillowing her head on his jacket.

Rising over her, Jeb brushed a leaf from her hair with a tenderness belying the violence of his kiss. "Will you be afraid?"

She moistened her dry lips with her tongue and found she tasted of brandy. Jeb wouldn't let any harm come to her. "Not as long as you're near."

He smiled and touched the bridge of her nose. He couldn't see the scar, but he knew it was there. He knew how she'd gotten it. She hadn't been afraid then, when he was with her. She was a brave lady, braver than she knew. Kissing her forehead, he whispered, "Hold that thought, sweetheart, and I'll be back before you know it."

Then he was gone, fading into a wall of black.

Sweat beading her face, Nicole lay frozen, daring to make no sound. She knew where he was going and why. And she was afraid, but for Jeb, not herself. Beneath the canyon like darkness of the magnolia, silences were deeper, magnifying tiny sounds until the soft rustle of trampled grass returning to normal posture became the thundering tick of a monstrous clock keeping time at a tortoise's pace.

Every second was an eon, each minute immeasurable, as she listened and waited.

And waited.

"Nicole! Nicole! Please, Nicole!"

The scream she'd dreaded had her scrambling to her feet. Coming from everywhere, and nowhere, echoing in her mind, the terror of it clawed at her spine like a serrated blade. The voice that screamed for her was deep, but immature. A child whose voice had grown when he had not.

"No. No. No. Jeb, no." She was running. Limbs grabbed at her hair and her clothes. Vines clawed at her, threatened to trip her. But she wouldn't allow it. Couldn't.

She stopped to orient herself. She had no sense of direction, no beacon to guide her.

A second scream filled the night, sliding down the scale to a plaintive whimper. A terrified child cried. One who wouldn't know his own strength, and Jeb wouldn't understand.

Precious seconds had been lost. She would be too late.
In anguish she whispered his name.
The name of a child.
"Ashley."

Five

The plaintive mewling of a frightened child finally stopped. But the hurt reflected in faded, watery eyes still haunted Jeb. No matter where he turned, their bewildered innocence followed him. Even in the dark, with the moon a glimmering golden globe, and night winds bearing the beguiling balm of the sea, they lay in wait to accuse.

Lifting his hands before his face, he stared at them. In the broken light falling from Nicole's bedroom door they were normal hands, of a normal man. Nothing about them appeared dangerous, certainly not lethal. But appearances deceived. As he deceived, and little more than an hour before, with only these damnable hands he had nearly throttled a child.

God help him, in any interpretation, a child.

The pad of Nicole's bare feet whispered over the deck. Another incongruity to be added to her dirtied and disheveled dinner finery. Her subtle fragrance drifted about him as she came to stand by his side.

The one constant in a bizarre evening.

Jeb's hands dropped to the deck rail, gripping. "How is he?"

"Asleep, finally."

"No." Jeb's head jerked. "I mean how is he, really?"

"Bruised. His throat will be sore for a while. And his ribs." Nicole touched his arm, feeling the tension in muscles and nerve. "He'll heal."

"Physically."

"And emotionally." Her fingers stroked his taut forearm. "Ashley won't remember. He never does."

"I don't think this is quite the same." Jeb knew the story of Ashley Blackmon. During the drive to the island, as she cradled the shuddering, hulking body with her own, Nicole told of a shy and gentle giant with the mind of a child. A wanderer of the streets of Charleston, considered a mild nuisance by some, a perfect target for malicious pranks by others.

"There was no way you could know, Jeb."

No, there was no way he could have known. But that little salve for his conscience didn't silence the frantic squall of terror that echoed in his mind. As long as he lived, he would feel that powerful body beneath his hands, and hear the frenzied cry for the only person Ashley Blackmon trusted.

Nicole.

"If anyone is to blame, then I am," she insisted gently.

"How do you figure that? You didn't burst through shrubs like Rambo, or garrote anyone." Jeb flexed his fingers, and found hers lacing through them, risking their steely grip.

"You aren't Rambo," she lifted their joined hands to the light. "And this is not a garrote. You did what any strong man would do. That it came down to that drastic measure is my fault and mine alone. I should have realized it might be Ashley." But her mind had been too full of Jeb to think of anyone, or anything else. "I didn't, and for that I will always blame myself."

"Why was he on the street at that hour? Why slinking from shadow to shadow?"

"Ashley is always on the street. He sleeps very little. When he saw us enter the park he was curious, even a little worried for me. He moved from hiding place to hiding

place, watching us, meaning to protect me if I needed it."
Her voice quavered then steadied, her hand tightened over
Jeb's. "As you did."

"The man needs a keeper," Jeb growled. "Someone to
protect *him*."

"There's no one."

"Then he should be sent to an institution, some place for
people like him."

"He has been. When he was much younger a group of
well-meaning citizens who felt just as you do, did what they
thought was the kindest thing. Ashley very nearly didn't
survive it. He's a wild creature that would rather die than
live in a cage. Even a comfortable cage. He'd never been
considered a threat to anyone, and no one wanted his death
laid at their door. So, the order for mandatory confine-
ment was reversed and he was allowed to return to the
streets. He's been a fixture there since I came to Charleston.

"I met him here in the park. I know now that was unusual. Ashley runs away from strangers. I'd been in Charleston a month, and I was lonely. He sensed it. It was a
common bond we shared."

"How did you discover he could paint?"

"Quite by accident. He left a bouquet of flowers at the
back door of the gallery. I wanted to give something in return. I don't know why I chose watercolors. I certainly had
no inkling of his talent...until I saw the first seascape."

A whimper from the bedroom sent Nicole rushing to
Ashley. She'd given him her room because it opened to the
deck, and the sea and he would feel less hemmed in. As she
knelt by his side, soothing him as he slept, she was more
aware of his enormous size than she'd ever been. He
dwarfed the familiar room, making ordinary things seem
small, and strange and close. For the first time, she understood his abnormal fear of houses. Walls closed him in.
Roofs shut out the sky, the sun and the stars.

With a child's concept of his size, he understood only that
rooms were tiny boxes that cramped and contained him. Yet
someone somewhere had recognized the greatest danger of
his size, and had taught him to be unfailingly gentle. Nicole

had seen the taunts and blows of bullies suffered with the same stoic patience that coaxed wounded birds and wild creatures like himself to his wondering hand.

Jeb had not needed force to subdue Ashley, but he couldn't be faulted for what he didn't know.

As she rose from the floor to look at the sleeping man, Jeb turned away from the door. He'd watched and listened as she offered solace. Whatever her feelings, or her thoughts, her touch was assuring, her voice serene.

From the moment she'd burst through the underbrush, catching at his arm, dragging him from the cowering, crying man, her concern had been for Ashley. The stab of anger it provoked in Jeb was shocking. Until he understood about Ashley, and then himself.

As he backed away from the door, the essence of a deeper, more far reaching understanding took root. No matter his size, no matter the strength buried in the massive body, Ashley was a child. Nicole had dealt with his fear and his need with an uncanny composure, on a level he could comprehend. She knew by instinct what to say, how to reassure him and comfort him.

An instinct that could only be borne of compassion and caring.

Suddenly everything was falling into place. What Jeb hoped and wanted to believe were merging into a single truth.

He needed to see her. He needed to look into her face, into her eyes.

God! He needed to know.

With an angry gesture he raked his hair back from his forehead. His mouth was a grim slash in his face. A muscle rippled in his cheek from the force of his clenched teeth. Every nerve keened for the sound of her step on the wooden boards of the deck. Every sinew of his body coiled and knotted with his struggle to wait for her to come to him.

Patience was one of his strengths. In The Watch it had to be. Tonight the last shred of it deserted him. He was turning to seek her out when she stepped through the doorway. As before, her step was a whisper, her fragrance blended with the night. Coiled and knotted sinew coiled and knotted even tighter.

"It was just a dream. He never really woke up," she explained.

"You like him, don't you?" Jeb looked down at her. She was small, but size hadn't mattered when she was needed.

"Of course."

"And children."

"Doesn't everyone?"

It was a rhetorical response, one of the meaningless, offhand comments people make. He knew it was far from an expression of what she believed, but it gave him the opening he needed.

"No, Nicole, not everyone." With the tips of his fingers he lifted her chin. His gaze ranged over her face, the strong line of her jaw, the sensual curve of her lips, the battle scar at the bridge of her nose. Her eyes. Lovely, guileless eyes. "There are people who do unspeakable things to children. Some claim it's in the name of love, others don't even bother with the lie. Ashley was afraid of me tonight, and afraid for you because he'd been taught to be afraid. Would you say his teachers love children?"

A bleak look washed over her face. Bitterness normally alien to her wrenched her heart as she recalled the pack of teens who, for no reason than the sick, inhuman thrill of it, had thrown gasoline on Ashley and struck a match. If she hadn't been in the park... If the fountain had been dry...

The horror of what might have been, the cruelty made her shudder even now. These were Ashley's teachers. There had been others.

Jeb waited with a new lease on patience. When he thought she wouldn't answer, her gaze lifted to his. "I hate it," she said in a tight voice.

Dark lashes half shielded eyes clouded with anguish and fierce anger. Yet her eyes were lovelier for the anguish and anger. Lovelier than anything Jeb Tanner had ever seen in his life.

"I hate what people do to each other, to their children and innocents like Ashley." Slashing an impotent hand through the darkness, she sighed and shook her head. "I hate it each time another story of a lost child is blazoned over the papers." Her voice dropped to a hoarse undertone. "But more than anything, I hate it when we're left to agonize over the last hours of a suffering child.

"Sometimes I wish..." She stopped and looked away. "I'm sorry." Catching her lower lip momentarily between her teeth to stem the outburst, she shook her head again. "I didn't mean to go off on a tangent. You ask a simple question, expecting a simple answer, and get a tirade instead."

"Don't be sorry, sweetheart." He curled a hand about the nape of her neck, his thumb stroking the incredibly smooth skin beneath her jaw. He'd gotten more than a tirade, more than a simple answer. Drawing a deep breath he felt the worry and fear fall away like iron chains. "Don't ever be sorry for caring."

He knew. Thank God, he knew.

Nicole would never hurt a child, or anyone. Nor forgive one who did. From this minute, and for always, he would stake his life on it.

Muttering unintelligibly—a groan, a curse, a prayer, not even he knew—he pulled her to him. And drew yet another long, ragged breath when she came willingly to his embrace.

With his arms wrapped tightly about her, his cheek resting against her hair, he savored the moonlit darkness, the constant rumble of the tide, wishing he could preserve their harmony for another time. For he was certain beyond any doubt the day would come when he must do exactly as he'd pledged, and risk his life for what he believed.

Jeb wiped sweat from his forehead and shaded his eyes as he looked to the top of the ruin. When he'd begun his run down the beach, Nicole was only a splash of color against gleaming marble, and Ashley was nowhere in sight. From his watchtower he recognized the familiar jeans, faded and worn nearly threadbare, but not the oversized T-shirt so outrageously orange it rivaled the sun. A stalking tiger appliquéd across the front was as lifelike as a photograph.

If she and Ashley hadn't been the only early risers on the beach, the flash of neon would have been his beacon as Nicole scampered about building sand castles and gathering shells to skim over the sand. They were two children reveling in an unaccustomed freedom, until a race to the ruin sent the lumbering Ashley stumbling into her.

Nicole had pulled up lame with a trickle of blood at her knee, then spent quite some time consoling Ashley. Finally she'd waved him away to play, while she climbed the ruin to keep her vigil over him.

Jeb laid his glasses aside then, deciding it was past time to make it a party of three.

"Good morning," he called up to her now, remembering this was the elegant woman who had come to him willingly on a moonlit deck, drawing solace of her own from his arms. Sandy and tousled, her beachcomber's clothing spattered with saltwater, she was no less woman.

No less desirable.

"Got an early start, I see." There was a soft edge in his voice, a huskiness he didn't expect.

"Ashley's an early riser." She smiled down at him, then looked at the cloudless sky. "Nice day for jogging."

"Yeah." Jeb tilted his head toward a faraway pool of water trapped in a sandy basin when the tide receded. "Better yet for splashing through ponds."

"He's been at it for nearly an hour now." And she with him, but now she was content to sit however long Ashley found the sand and water amusing.

"How is he?"

"Better every minute."

"Now that I'm not around, you mean."

Nicole had no answer, no explanation for Ashley's unusual mood. "I don't know what's gotten into him. He's never behaved like this before."

Jeb had sat with her, keeping vigil over the restless manchild through the first night. The next day Ashley had been agitated, given to spurts of sulking interspersed with fits of crying. He rarely ever spoke, but after racking her brain for reasons, Nicole finally sensed his silences were related to Jeb.

For Ashley's peace of mind, but only after her steadfast assurances that Ashley would die before he would hurt her, Jeb backed off.

He'd needed some time to touch base with Mitch and Matthew, and to report to Simon. For the first time in a long while, his report hadn't been as complete as it might have been. Simon was a brainstormer who believed in gut instinct. But only as a beginning. Then he expected concrete evidence to back it up.

Jeb had not discussed his certainty that Nicole knew nothing of Tony's life or his crimes. He wouldn't. Not yet. Not until her path crossed with Matthew Sky.

He would arrange it soon, perhaps in Charleston. Something casual, innocuous. As Matthew's not-by-chance gossipy and unproductive encounter with Mrs. Atherton at a rival gallery had been. "How long before you plan to return to the gallery?" Jeb asked. "Annabelle must be missing you."

"We're going back today." She looked from Jeb to Ashley who was coaxing a small sandpiper to his hand. "He likes the island, but he's beginning to miss his routine."

"You think he'll be all right now?"

"I'm sure of it. Ashley has remarkable recuperative powers. His biggest problem now is that he's feeling caged in and homesick. He slept on the deck last night, and nothing I could say could dissuade him. He argues brilliantly, by simply refusing to hear what he doesn't want to hear, or turning it around."

"Have you ever wondered how much he understands?"

"I'm convinced it varies with the subject and the situation. Whether he's calm or disturbed, or even tired."

"You know him pretty well, don't you?"

"We've been friends for years."

Only days ago she'd confessed there were no men in her life. She'd been too busy for romance, yet she'd taken time to befriend a mentally and emotionally handicapped man. Once Jeb would have sneered and wondered if she were a candidate for plaster sainthood or the worst sort of liar. Now he accepted her words, and what he saw, as unpretentious truth.

"You're going this morning?"

Nicole shifted on hard stone, pointing a narrow, sneaker-clad foot to ease a cramping calf. "As soon as Ashley is ready. He loathes cars, so I thought it would be best to let him enjoy the morning first. Annabelle has been pinch-hitting for me at the gallery. She says coping with Mrs. Atherton part of one more day won't kill her."

"But what about the reverse?"

Nicole laughed and bent to rub her bare leg below the raveling bottom of cutoff jeans. "They're frauds, both of them. All bark, no bite."

"I wish I were as sure of that as I am that you're not going to be able to climb down from there with that leg like it is."

"No problem." She dismissed his concern. "It's just a cramp."

"So I see." What he saw was the muscles of her calf knotted and drawn, her toes curling back to the arch of her foot. "You could walk it off."

"Not yet." Dark hair flew in ebony strands about her face as she bent to flex her foot. "Ashley feels safer if he can see me here."

"All right. If you're not coming down..." Jeb scaled toppled walls and nearly vertical remains of roof and floor as if he'd been doing it all his life. At the top of the ten-foot heap of stone, he stood looking out over the shore, then dropped down beside her. "Now, let's see to that leg."

"Thanks, but it isn't necessary." Nicole wasn't really sure she wanted him touching her. Not now, not here. Not when the sun glinted on his bare arms, reminding her how good it felt to let him hold her. Not when the sense of peace she'd found in his embrace was only a small part of what she wanted and needed.

What she needed now was to keep her wits about her, to deal sensibly with Ashley, and Jeb had a way of making her forget to be sensible. Tucking the offending leg beneath the other, she fought for a reassuring smile as the convulsing muscle closed into a tighter knot of agony.

"I'm fine." She didn't hear the raggedness of her voice, nor see the lines between her brows. "Really."

"Sure you are," Jeb agreed, taking a page from Ashley's book of passive argument. "As fine as you were the day Tony's surfboard smacked you across the nose and left you with a couple of temporary shiners and a permanent scar."

"That was a long time ago. A lot has changed."

"Yes, it has. So don't be stubborn, one child on the beach is enough for now." Before she could demur again, he lifted her leg to his lap and stripped away her sneaker. "Relax," he urged. "It's no wonder this happened, you're tense as a brick."

She wanted to tell him a brick wasn't tense and neither was she, but his fingers were sliding the length of her calf, working magic that was half torment, half pleasure. For one fleeting moment she fell beneath their ambivalent spell. Then he found the muscle in spasm, and with his hand fisted, kneaded it with his knuckles.

Nicole gasped and tried to twist away from the shock of excruciating pain lancing from toe to knee. She heard his low curse and an apology muttered under his breath, but he didn't release her.

"No!" Her hand closed over his shoulder, her nails scoring the hard, taut skin beneath his damp shirt. She meant to demand that he stop, but the demand died in her throat, as she realized the pain stopped instead.

The long muscle, that had been like a stone for what seemed an eternity, relaxed. Jeb's touch gentled. His dancing fingers ranged from her knee to her toes, following the path of her pain, discovering tiny aches she didn't know existed.

Nicole couldn't fight anymore. She didn't try. Bracing against her forearms, she leaned back and raised her face to an endless azure sky. As she moaned softly in relief, as tension and misgiving eased, her eyes closed shuttering away all the world but Jeb.

His exploring hands were more than gentle, more than magic. They were comfort and healing. And bewitching.

The surf whispered at low tide. An early morning sun warmed but didn't burn. The first hint of a breeze teased over her skin with the sensuality of a lover's kiss. Nicole drifted. Content, and yet . . . not.

Slowly, so slowly she was barely sentient of it, an awareness crept into her reverie. A subtle move, a breath not drawn. Restraint in a heated touch. The boding of longings unrealized.

Words left unsaid.

Words of passion and need.

A dream. She was only dreaming.

And in a beautiful, waking dream, in his silence, Jeb Tanner wanted Nicole Callison as much as she wanted him.

A dream. Only a dream.

A gull swooped low, his strident beggar's cry and the rush of his wings shattering their little inlet of quiet. Nicole stirred restlessly under Jeb's ministrations, her mind reaching for a lost illusion. When she knew it was gone, she smiled a wistful smile for what couldn't be.

"Better?" Jeb didn't take his hand from the smooth arch of her foot. He'd watched as the easing of pain had drawn her down, centered her thoughts, calming her until the weariness she denied was gone.

"Better?" she murmured. "Yes. Infinitely." Dark lashes fluttered against her cheeks with the effort to drag her eyes open. She felt as if she'd slept, long and deeply, for hours. When she looked at him her gaze was serene, but far, far beyond it, so far she thought no one would ever see, lay a shadow of regret.

He wanted to take her in his arms and soothe her until there was only sunlight in her eyes. But he dared not, for it would only be a beginning. A public beach that would be far from deserted in only a few minutes was not the place for beginnings.

But there was a place for beginnings, with a house built, as Folly's ruin had been, as a gift of love. Where walks were carefully tended and flowers planted more for texture and scent than color. Where lost children, a girl and a boy, shared forever a treasure from the sea. And deserted beaches were truly deserted.

"I don't remember the last time I felt so rested."

Eden.

"I would ask where you learned your skill, Mr. Tanner, but I'm not sure I really want to know."

If the time was ever right, he would take her there.

"I think you've worked a miracle."

For now he would bide his time and play the game.

And hope.

"No miracle, sweetheart." He tousled her hair as he had when she was fifteen, and laughed as he bent to get her shoe. "I don't have the right credentials for that."

"I would argue that point, but it would take too much effort."

"And I would argue that you need a lot more sleep and a tall glass of orange juice."

Orange juice, for potassium. The surfers' way of avoiding cramps by putting back one of the elements the sun sucked from their bodies. "I'll see to both," she promised. "As soon as Ashley is . . . Ashley!"

She bounded to her feet, one shod, one bare. "Where is he?"

"Exactly where he was five minutes ago," Jeb assured her calmly.

"Five minutes?" She couldn't believe such a short interval had passed.

"He almost had the sandpiper, at the last second it shied away. But it's only a matter of time."

Scanning the shore, she found Ashley crouched in the sand, patiently waiting for the tiny bird to return.

"He's going to be covered with sand. Maybe I should help him bathe before you go into the city."

Nicole made a dismissive gesture. "That won't be necessary. He does that scrupulously himself. Someone taught him very well. Clothing has been a problem, of course, but I can brush most of the sand off."

"He seems to know so much. Who taught him, Nicole? And when?"

"His mother, I assume, but she's as much a mystery as everything else about him. He calls himself Blackmon, but no one knows if it's really true. In fact, no one can find any family connections at all."

"How old is he? Where did he come from?"

"He could be fifty, or a bit more. The woman simply appeared on the streets fifty years or so ago. The last forty he's been alone."

"He was just a kid!"

Nicole agreed. "Ten. Maybe a little younger. Maybe a little older."

"Why didn't someone do something then?"

"I don't think anyone realized he was alone at first. He was more reclusive then, and not so big. The pattern of his life was set before his situation became apparent. Then it was too late. Trying to place him in an institution proved that."

"You've tried to find someone for him, haven't you?"

She didn't bother denying or admitting what had been apparent. "Maybe I was a fool to try when no one else had succeeded, and after so many years, but I felt he needed someone to belong to. A place, a family. Roots." A defeated shrug of her shoulders eloquently described the futility of her search. "As I said, I was a fool, on a fool's errand."

Jeb caught her wrist, his fingers circling the small, delicate bones as he drew her back to his side. "Not a fool's errand." His fingers skimmed over her bare arm to her shoulder and the collar of her shirt. Gathering the bright fabric in his fists, he drew her close. "Not a fool."

"Jeb..."

"A lady," he murmured, ignoring her feeble protest, "searching for the gift of happiness for someone she cared about."

"Jeb..."

He stopped her with a kiss. Chaste, simple, the kiss of a friend. It would have to do for now. Backing away he nodded to Ashley who stood at the base of the ruin glaring at them. "I think you'd better put on your shoe, Ashley is ready to go back to Charleston."

"It's just as well. The first of the thundering herd just arrived." Gaudy umbrellas were springing up on the beach like toadstools after a rain. Sliding her foot into her shoe she made quick work of the laces and climbed down to shore.

Ashley seemed nervous. Worry carved the lines of his face deeper, and pale eyes darted from Nicole, to Jeb and back again. Nicole patted his shoulder. "Don't be afraid. No one will tease you here."

Massive shoulders shrugged, shaggy hair flew as he shook his head violently.

"What's wrong, Ashley? What's bothering you?"

"Hurt." His voice was rusty but the word was clear.

"Where?" Nicole was instantly concerned. "Is it your throat? Your ribs?"

The violent shake again. "You."

"Me? Ashley, there's nothing— My knee!" She'd wiped away the blood, but the small scratch was raw and angry. "It's fine, Ashley, truly. When we crashed into each other you didn't hurt me."

"Good." His acceptance of her assurance didn't seem to ease his concern. A hand the size of a ham lifted to her face. Sand-covered fingers touched her lips tentatively, carefully. "Hurt?"

As a rule Nicole needed only a word or a gesture to be on the same wavelength with Ashley. Then communication became a jumble of single words, intuition and mind reading. But this time her assumption was so far from the mark, she was a minute reassimilating it.

Jeb was there before her, interpreting mildly, "He's asking if I hurt you when I kissed you. I think he suspects that I did."

Or that he would.

"Of course it didn't hurt." Nicole caught both huge hands in hers, ignoring the sand. "No more than it does when I kissed your cheek. You do remember when I kissed you, don't you?"

Ashley stared at their hands and shook his head.

"You brought flowers to the gallery and I kissed you."

"Why?"

"It's something people do when they like someone."

"Me." Ashley slipped a hand free to thump himself on the chest. His colorless gaze wandered from Nicole to Jeb. His fist thudded again. "Me."

This time Nicole's perceptions were on target. Anyone would have understood. "I like you, Ashley. We're friends. We always will be, but Jeb's a friend, too. I've known him for a long time."

"No!" The big man turned away, his scowl a perfect replica of a pouting three-year-old.

"Yes!" Nicole went to stand in front of him, lifting his bowed head, forcing him to look at her. "That doesn't mean I like you any less than I always have. We all like more than one thing, or one person."

"No."

"Of course we do. Even you."

"No." A pouting lip trembled.

"You like chickadees. Does that mean you can't like herons, too?"

"Like herons."

"I know you do. You like Annabelle, too, don't you?"

"Funny lady."

"Annabelle is funny and you like that. But you don't stop liking me because you like Annabelle, do you?"

"No." There was a quaver in the unpracticed voice, and tears on quivering unshaven cheeks.

Nicole brushed away a tear, as if he were truly three. "Would it make you feel better if I kissed you?"

"Yes."

Solemnly, Nicole rose on tiptoe and, grasping his face in her palms she drew him down to her. As lovingly as a mother, she kissed one eye then the other and moved away. "There, is that better?"

"Better." Rising from her grasp, over her head, Ashley's gaze blazed into Jeb's. "Two."

The word was harsh, fierce, its meaning unmistakable. Jeb bowed his head and conceded. "Two."

Ashley was satisfied, Jeb and his one kiss didn't matter, and were forgotten for the moment. "Like kitty."

"Oh, you do, do you?" Nicole glanced down at the tiger on her shirt. "You could paint one even prettier."

"Nope." The pout was back.

"Oh, yes." Nicole took Ashley's hand again, leading him down the beach toward her house as she spoke. "I know what we'll do. Since you like kitties, one day soon we'll plan a trip to the zoo.''

''Zoo?''

''It's a place where animals are kept. Unusual animals like kitty here. You'll like it.''

''Like Nicole. Like Annabelle. Like chickadee. Like heron. Like kitty.''

''I know.'' This, for Ashley, was veritable chattering. Nicole had rarely heard him say so much. ''I know something else.''

''What?''

''One day you might like Mr. Tanner.''

''Tanner?'' Ashley stopped, dragging at her hand. ''Tanner?''

''Jeb,'' she explained.

''No.'' His response was instant, unequivocal and sparing no glance for Jeb.

Nicole sighed and scuffed her feet in the sand, temporarily defeated by the childlike doggedness.

Ashley sighed and scuffed his feet in a perfect imitation, immediately intrigued by this new game.

Laughing in her defeat, Nicole tugged him down the beach, swinging their clasped hands between them. Ashley's good mood was restored. Not daring the risk of another mercurial change, without turning she wagged the fingers of her free hand over her shoulder.

A goodbye salute for Jeb.

Jeb grinned at the jaunty wave. Nicole was as much diplomat as she was compassionate friend.

Ashley didn't look back. Jeb didn't expect he would. The poor man was mildly retarded, but the erratic swing of his interest and his moods didn't mean he didn't think and feel, and hurt deeply.

''Poor fella.'' He mused, speaking his thoughts as Nicole led the troubled giant to a staircase leading over the dune. Jeb's mouth turned down in an wry smile. Ashley had just learned another painful lesson, and Jeb understood, for he'd learned the same lesson himself in Waterfront Park, when Nicole called another man's name.

There was a lot he hadn't understood then. A lot that made it easy to forgive. But he wouldn't forget.

Jealousy hurt. It hurt like hell.

"I can't believe Jeb did that." Annabelle's eyebrows threatened to disappear into her hairline all over again.

Nicole had gone over this before and she was weary of it. With faltering patience she explained one more time. "He didn't understand about Ashley."

"Why didn't you tell him?"

"Annabelle!" Nicole lost her battle with frustration. She'd dropped Ashley off at the park and come directly to the gallery. Since then her assistant had asked thousands of questions. At least it seemed like thousands. Struggling to regain her patience she said, "I didn't know it was Ashley."

"Why didn't you?" Annabelle asked, choosing to ignore the edge in Nicole's voice. "He's always in the park, and if you're around, he's always following you."

"I was distracted. It just didn't occur to me."

"It didn't occur! The man's your shadow, and it didn't occur to you?"

"Please." Nicole rubbed an aching temple with her fingertips. "Can we just drop it? Forget it ever happened?"

"All right. Fine." Short arms folded over a massive bosom. "I can, if you can." Bright, birdlike eyes watched her. "Can you?"

"Of course I can."

"Good, then we both will."

"Good."

"I said that." Annabelle still studied her closely. She'd known Nicole far too long not to realize there was more to this than simple mistaken identity and a scuffle in the park. More to Nicole's reaction. More to Jeb Tanner, who laughed at the suggested mystery in his past and his present.

"So you did." With a dismissive bearing Nicole walked away from the probing scrutiny. There was much to be done to catch up for her days away from the gallery. She tried to concentrate. Tried to judge artists and their work as it deserved to be judged. But at the oddest moments her thoughts drifted to Jeb in the moonlight.

"You left out that Ashley doesn't like Jeb, didn't you?"

Nicole didn't know why she'd left out the last part at the beach. Perhaps she should have known better. Annabelle was too astute not to surmise correctly, filling in the gaps left unexplained. Even now she was tempted to lie, but it would be futile. "You're right, Ashley doesn't like Jeb."

"Because you like him."

"Yes."

"More than as an old friend."

Nicole raked a hand through her hair and looked away. But even then she could feel the dark eyes pinioning her like a butterfly and a hat pin. She couldn't lie to Annabelle.

She couldn't lie to herself. Not anymore. "Yes, I like Jeb Tanner."

As she turned away she didn't see Annabelle's dark piercing gaze turn to concern. "I like him as more than an old friend." Then in a voice nearly too low to be heard, "Far more."

Six

"We've hardly discussed her brother except in a passing remark."

Jeb paced the floor, dragging the telephone cord behind him, explaining to Simon that beyond their first intense meetings, his contact with Nicole had been regular for the most part, but brief and casual. An unprompted opportunity to broach the subject hadn't occurred.

In the interim he'd discovered Nicole was singularly the least curious person he'd ever known. A rare listener, not one to question and as reticent about her personal life as if she'd spent her adulthood in deep cover. A condition and trait common to The Black Watch. Men like himself.

"Timing is critical, certainly. Tony's already taken longer to make contact than expected. That means he'll come soon. I understand what I have to do."

With each blunt answer Jeb's irritation was mounting. Simon McKinzie wouldn't fail to take note, but it wouldn't change anything.

Tony Callison was still at large. Still a conscienceless killer, and Jeb Tanner was still the one man who might stop him.

By whatever means necessary.

"No, sir, I haven't taken the *Gambler* out. I'm aware that's inconsistent with the image I've cultivated here on the island. And yes, sir, I suppose it would be safe to assume Nicole would go for a sail."

He waited, with little forbearance, through Simon's reminder of how critical Nicole and her unwitting cooperation were to the operation. He'd heard it endlessly before he came to the island. He heard it now in every thought and every nightmare.

"Yes, I said assume." Barely controlled anger bristled beneath his even tone. "I can only assume, Simon, because I haven't asked."

He didn't bother to admit that he couldn't predict how an invitation to spend a day sailing would be received because he hadn't made direct contact with Nicole since the morning after the incident on the beach with Ashley.

Four days since then. Seven since he'd kissed her in the park. Seven since he'd held her in the moonlight.

Simon was pressing a valid point. There was no escaping the urgency.

"Yes, sir. I'll see to it, sir," Jeb responded curtly.

Moving to the window he looked out at the shore. There were dozens of sunbathers and beach walkers braving the morning heat, but for Jeb the shore was deserted.

"Say again." He turned his back on the window, forgetting to tack the pointed respect to his blunt command. "Eden?"

The receiver was a rock in his hand, heavy, cold. He'd thought of taking Nicole to Eden one day. In a moment of delusion when he'd hoped some remnant of respect for him would survive, he'd thought of Eden. He'd never stopped to consider why, only that he had.

Tamped anger flared at the synchronous direction of thoughts not uncommon among The Black Watch. At Simon for suggesting Patrick McCallum's island paradise be sullied once more by The Black Watch. At himself for thinking the impossible.

Nothing could survive betrayal.

"Yes, sir," Jeb snapped in his distraction. "I'm listening. A sail to the island should be conducive to discussion. I understand. The island is unoccupied, Patrick knows we will be there." In a redundant, word-for-word repetition of all his grizzled commander said, he made clear he knew he'd been given a direct command. A tired flex of his shoulders marked his reluctant compliance to this isolated and uncustomary interference. "This weekend should work. Yes," he said grimly, "today. But first, I have a favor to ask. One you owe me."

A half hour later the receiver was back in its cradle. The last part of their conversation on the secured line had nothing to do with Eden, and only indirectly with Nicole. The details he'd given Simon were sketchy, the favor nearly impossible, but if he were going to draw her deeper into the betrayal of her brother, Jeb meant her to have something left that mattered.

He paced again, unaware of the pristine luxury that fit the affluent life-style he'd assumed. Splashes of subtle color intended to please the eye, didn't please his. He had no sense of spaciousness. The stylistic mood of harmony sought by hue and design seemed more than contrived.

The house was too close, too sterile. The room was a box, its walls and lofty ceilings a cage. The sky and the sea were far more enticing.

Something more he and Ashley shared, in part.

Simon, the canny Scot, was right as always. It was past time he took the *Gambler* out.

If his destination must be Eden, then Eden it would be.

"Perfect." Annabelle backed to her desk and her chair, to gain a better perspective of the miniatures she'd been arranging, and to rest her feet. As her shoes hit the floor she groaned and wiggled her bare toes. After a critical study she still agreed with her first assessment. Matted, framed and placed against an especially prepared wall, the paintings were startling.

"Yes!" She crowed with a triumphant pump of her hand. A gesture worthy of the most volatile tennis pro. "It was a stroke of genius for you to take Ashley to the zoo," she said, sharing with largesse the credit for the display. "He must have painted like a demon this week to do four. He does animals as well as birds and ships. A little water, a little color, a squiggle or two on canvas, and *voilà!* A masterpiece."

Nicole didn't agree or disagree, she was too engrossed in draping a length of rough woven cloth over a table, weaving it around small bronze sculptures.

"It was a stroke of genius, as well, to group Hunter Slade's newest work with Ashley's paintings." Another stroke was Beth Slade persuading her husband to allow the animals he carved for their son to be cast.

Nicole positioned a small tiger beneath Ashley's painting of the same animal, a majesty captured as flawlessly on canvas as bronze. Absently she dragged her attention from her chore. "I'm sorry, I wasn't listening."

"Ha!" Annabelle jangled a bank of silver bangles stretching from her wrist to the middle of her arm. "You haven't listened to a fraction of what I've said for the past week."

"I'm listening now."

"You haven't listened since the escapade with Ashley and your fella." Nicole's interruption went unnoticed, now that the smaller woman had an opening to make known her observations. Again. "He hasn't been around lately, has he?"

"You know he hasn't."

"Hmm, I wonder why."

"It could be because he's busy." Nicole would never in this lifetime let Annabelle suspect that she'd spent more hours than she wanted to admit asking the same question.

"He's retired, remember." An innocent lift of eyebrows fooled no one, still Annabelle played the part.

"Only from a nine-to-five position." Nicole moved a length of cloth, gathering it about a moss-covered stone she'd fetched from a creek near the island. "Considering his life-style, and because he has retired, I imagine he has financial matters to attend to. And he isn't my fella, as you call him." The rebuke was given mildly and without a prayer of halting the discussion that was inevitable.

"But you like him," Annabelle persisted.

"Liking Jeb doesn't make him more than a friend."

"But you'd like him even more as more than a friend." This gibberish was delivered with a sage and knowing look.

"We've been through this before, almost word for word, Annabelle." There was a somber disquiet in Nicole's expression conflicting with her reserved manner. "It doesn't matter what I feel, or don't feel. Jeb's a friend. Period. End of story, and it's for the best exactly that way."

She moved the cloth again, sighed and shook her head. "He's restless already. One day he'll sail away and that will be that. Who knows how many years might pass before I would see him again. If ever. So—" she glanced back, her own brow lifted over a cool stare "—let's drop it, shall we?"

"He's restless, all right, but not because he plans to leave." Annabelle drummed her fingers thoughtfully on her desk, ignoring the subtle warning. "There's something about him. Something that doesn't quite fit. As if he isn't who he says he is, or what he pretends to be."

Nicole laughed, a humorless sound. "Jeb is Jeb. Not a wolf in sheep's clothing."

"You've got that much right. He's a wolf in wolf's clothing."

"Ahh, but you like wolves, remember?"

"Of course, I do. But I like this one, especially." It bothered the chatty woman not one whit that her declaration should have been at odds with her suspicions. Such mundane sensibility never occurred to Annabelle. "In fact, I like him almost as much as you do."

"Annabelle!" The rebuke was softly given, despite the edge that crept into it. And, as before, it was of absolutely no consequence.

"What is it about mysterious bad boys that make us forget every caution as we tumble for them?" the woman prattled on.

Nicole picked up a winsome figure of a giraffe, knelt by the table, scowled, then set it back in precisely the same spot. The display was a jumble, her mind was a world away from aesthetic order. "For the last time," she snapped as she stared blindly at Hunter Slade's clever menagerie. "Jeb isn't a boy, he isn't bad and, if he's mysterious it's because he just doesn't talk about himself."

"That's an understatement. He arrives here, sailing from out of China for all we know. He has a beautiful boat, a gorgeous crew straight out of *GQ*, or whatever that ritzy male fashion magazine is called. Wow! Talk about wolves!" Annabelle rolled her eyes heavenward. "A whole pack of them. All untamed, all gorgeous.

"So money is obviously no object." After the lusty digression, she was back on track. "Not with his boat, not with his crew and certainly not when he buys the most fabulous house on the beach. Then he settles into becoming one of the boys, but only at first. Now he doesn't bar hop, he doesn't golf, he doesn't play tennis. Most peculiar of all, he doesn't sail.

"He listens well, though," Annabelle added thoughtfully. "So well, he never talks. Everyone seems to know *of* him, but no one really knows *him*."

"You've been gossiping again." Nicole managed to insert her own observation into the monologue.

"No, I've been listening, like he does." An adamant finger was leveled at Nicole. "Can you look me in the eye and deny what I've said? Can you tell me who knows anything about him? The fact is, no one does." Her dark eyes narrowed. "Not even you, I'm afraid."

The uncomfortable truth of Annabelle's commentary couldn't be denied. Nicole didn't try. Cradling her head in her hand she massaged her temples, but the tension didn't ease. "What would you have me do, Annabelle?" she asked wearily. "Stop seeing him?"

A rhetorical question, for, evidently, he'd stopped seeing her.

"And miss all the fun?" Annabelle hooted. "Mercy, no! The man's a seething inferno of sensuality. He reeks of sex appeal without intending it. It's part of him—in the way he walks, and moves and looks at a woman.

"At least, if that woman is you." She delivered this in a droll aside, then hurried on before Nicole could protest. "And the hell of it is, it's as natural to him as breathing and blond hair. If he could bottle it and sell it, he would be a millionaire."

"He is already," Nicole muttered with no hope of throttling the discourse.

"Maybe he knows what he has, maybe he doesn't, but that's neither here nor there. The bottom line is he has it, in spades. It smolders in him, like a banked fire waiting for that small spark. Then pow!" Bangles flew from wrist to elbow with another theatrical gesture. "Inferno!"

"So?" Nicole found there was some small satisfaction to be garnered from being deliberately obtuse.

"So!" Eyebrows lifted higher, threatening to disappear into a heart-shaped hairline. "My sweet innocent! Half the enjoyment in life is dancing too near the fire." The handsome face, with its perfect makeup, sobered. The drama was ended, she'd been serious before, now it was time to be deadly serious. "Flirt with the fire, darling. Feel the delicious heat. Savor it. Let it singe you, and scorch you. And please, look at yourself for once. See that you have the same sensuality. Recognize your sex appeal. Use it. Kindle fires of your own.

"*But*—" a beringed finger wagged, long hair flew with the vigor of emphasis "—never, never *ever* get burned."

Nicole's throat was dry. Annabelle had just suggested what she'd always dreamed of, but never dared. If she dared, if just this once she let go of the iron control she'd been a lifetime learning, if she risked heart and soul, and mind and body, for Jeb, what would she be when he left her?

Dear God! How would she survive?

"Annabelle, I can't." There was a desperateness in her, a need that frightened. "It's impossible."

"Yes, you can. Playing twinkle toes on a tightrope over an inferno is scary as hell and twice as exciting. But it can be done, I'm proof of it." A long breath lifted large breasts, threatening the décolletage of her Gypsy blouse. "And when it is..." A wistful look flitted over classic features. "Ahh, when it is the rewards are incomparable."

"I don't think I can dance as well as you," Nicole murmured wryly. "I don't know how."

The bangles were silent, one stubby but graceful hand folded over the other in a long-suffering attitude of a loving mother encouraging her diffident child. "You begin by believing nothing is impossible. Then you learn, my dear. You learn every delicious step of the dance. And, unless I've lost my judgment completely, you could have no better teacher than the wolf waiting by the door."

"The wolf by the . . ." Nicole bit back her retort. The air was suddenly charged. A heavy weight descended on her chest, but did nothing to still the erratic beat of her heart. She didn't need to turn to know who stood at the door. Vaguely, she remembered the single chiming of the bell. One note, not the whole repertoire, as if he'd silenced it, preferring no announcement of his arrival.

She climbed to her feet, not sure if she should be glad or sorry the morning had been slow and the gallery had no browsers. Turning her back on the exhibit that had troubled her all morning, she faced him. In a glance, days of worry and hurt vanished. All that mattered was that he was here.

"Hello, Jeb." There was a tremor in her voice and she fought to calm it.

"Good morning, Nicky." Beyond his greeting he said no more. He looked at her in silence, admiring the carefully groomed veneer. Beneath the perfect exterior there was no glimmer of the windblown hoyden who walked and played on the beach like a tomboy in a faded and artlessly alluring swimsuit. No hint of the deep well of passion and compassion underlying the calm.

No hint unless one looked deeply into eyes that could range the spectrum of blue and green and gray in accordance with what she wore. Or with her mood. Today her eyes caught the blue fire of her dress and smoldered with countless questions he couldn't answer.

He moved from the door farther into the gallery, stopping in unintentional irony by the massive figure of the wolf. His counterpart, leader of the pack, proud, handsome. A canny creature, perhaps more familiar with danger than security.

Nicole suppressed a shiver as she sensed their kinship. Disturbed that she'd fallen prey to Annabelle's fantasy, she lifted her chin, challenging her own weakness. But dealing with the cause was not so simple. When she'd seen him last he'd been dressed in running shorts and a light T-shirt. Sweat had gleamed on his body, soaking the nylon, catching it close, as if he'd just come from the sea. All that was missing was a surfboard tucked under his arm.

On that familiar territory, with Ashley as their common interest, she'd let herself believe the years hadn't passed and Jeb was the carefree friend and confidant she'd needed so desperately. He was what had been missing in her life for so long. The illusion was so credible she'd begun to feel comfortable with him and with his touch.

She'd felt safe.

Now she knew it was only an illusion. She'd known before she'd risen to face him. She'd known all along.

She would never be safe from Jeb. Never so long as she lived. Yet she had only herself to fear, for the danger lay within her. Deep in a heart that had loved him. A heart that loved him still.

She didn't need to be reminded that he'd changed, and become the man who stood before her. One glance etched his true image forever in her mind, dressed, as she'd rarely seen him, in elegantly tailored trousers and a casual shirt open at the neck. His perfectly groomed hair, grown shaggy in the week, had been slicked back but refused to stay, falling over his forehead in an unruly wave that cried out to be brushed into order.

Jeb's hair had always been thick and rich and unruly. Memory wouldn't be still as she recalled when he'd worn it to his shoulders for that reason, tying it at his nape long before the male ponytail was stylishly correct.

The child in her remembered the times she'd run her fingers through it, combing it back to secure it after a rogue wave had torn it from its cruel binding. Time and distance and maturity had long ago let her realize he hadn't needed her help, but suffered her delighted ministrations out of kindness.

Kindness had been as natural to him then as sensuality was today. As Annabelle presumed, as natural as breathing.

Nicole's mind shied away from that. She didn't want to think of kindness or sensuality. She didn't want to think about how attractive he'd been and was, nor about the long lazy look that swept over her now, leaving very little of her unexplored.

Her gaze didn't falter beneath the intriguing exploration. She wouldn't let anything betray her struggle to convince herself it was the power of a memory coupled with Annabelle's prattle of men of mystery and wolves that set her pulse tripping. Yes, she assured herself, only prattle. Her chin lifted a fraction higher as she realized it was left to her to break the silence stretching to an uncomfortable degree.

"What brings you to town?" She was inordinately pleased with the mundane query. Pleased that her voice was normal, not awkwardly cheerful. The voice of a woman who had made her place in the world, not the child who had first loved him.

"You, Nicole," he said softly, drawing his ranging gaze to her face. "You bring me to town."

Her hand drifted to her throat, then to a button at the fold of her dress. The lace of the customary chemise, only a sliver of blue peeking out in the intention of complementing rather than distracting, made total mockery of its purpose, and of the demure professional demeanor she'd adopted for her workday.

"I beg your pardon?" The button turned between her fingers, lace moved like a secret veil over the first delicate slope of her breasts.

"You, Nicole." He was moving toward her, stepping past the wolf, past the table and its array of tiny animals, wondering why he had waited so long. "I came for you."

Whatever she expected, it wasn't this—the heated look, the intensity in his voice.

"It's a splendid day," he continued as if he neither needed nor wanted a reply. "The sea is calm and the wind is perfect for sailing."

"You came to take me sailing?" Purposely or not, he was a master at keeping her off balance.

"That's exactly why I came."

"At eleven o'clock on a business day? Surely you're joking!"

"I never joke about sailing." He touched her cheek with the tip of a finger, allowing himself that little contact with the satin of her skin. "Surely you haven't forgotten."

"I haven't forgotten." She was wooden beneath the caress. She mustn't let herself fall to temptation. Oh yes, she was tempted, she wanted the wind in her hair and the spray of the sea on her face. She wanted to dance close to the fire and give herself up to its heat.

An old fear careened through her as she shook her head vehemently. "I can't."

The finger that trailed over her cheek slipped to her throat, dipping into the tiny well at its base. A roughened pad stroked the throbbing pulse, lazily, gently, then moved down, down, pausing only a heartbeat from the lace that intrigued and fascinated.

"Nicole," he murmured and waited. "Nicole." The marauding touch retraced its path, from pulse, to throat, to her chin to lift her face to his. His gaze reached into her, holding her. His hand slipped from her face to her hair, his fingers tangling tightly in it, as if he thought she would tear free of his grasp. "Why are you afraid, Nicole?"

"I'm not afraid. Not of you." A lie only by omission. Only in that it was half truth.

He frowned, truly perplexed. "Of sailing?"

"No."

"Then tell me."

Tell him what? The whole lie? The whole truth? Nicole chose neither as she took refuge in biting sarcasm. "I can't go with you, but it isn't because I'm afraid. You forget, not all of us are rich or retired. Some of us still need to work before we can play."

He refused to take offense, refused to back off. No matter what she said, he'd seen excitement in her eyes, then something else. If not fear, then something he must understand. But that would come later. "When do you play, Nicky?"

"I have a shop to run, I play when the work is done."

"When is that?" Before she could reply, he answered for her. "You give yourself one day—once in a while."

"It's enough."

Her face was so small and his hand so large, he could stroke the tender flesh beneath her eyes with his thumb and never release his hold on her hair. "If it's enough, why do I see fatigue here? Why does an encounter with Mrs. Atherton take more out of you than it should?"

Nicole wanted to move away. Far away from his touch, farther still from the soft, caressing voice. Yet neither would let her. Caring words and a feather-light touch held her as strongly as iron bands. "I do what I must. When I must. For as long as I must. There's no one else."

"There's Annabelle," he suggested. "And Ravenel. He helps most gladly when you need him, doesn't he? Either or both of them would be delighted for you to take some time away from the gallery."

"I've taken time off. Two days within the week."

"For Ashley, not for yourself." His hand tightened in her hair, with a need to shake her lofty composure, to kindle the leap of excitement he'd seen. "How long has it been since you've put the shackles of the world behind you?"

"That's impossible," she said unsteadily, a wistful note in her tone.

He hadn't looked away from her, he didn't now. His voice was low, intimate. "Nothing is impossible, and what better place to prove it than under sail with only the sea and the sky to hold you?"

"Don't, Jeb." Her hand closed over his wrist, a balance for the dizzy rush of desire that set her head spinning. He was seducing her, making her ache for things she couldn't have. For peace, for quiet, for space. For him.

His only answer was a smile, and Nicole realized he knew what he was doing. It was all part of a calculated plan. A swift, angry flush swept over her. She didn't like to be teased or manipulated.

Abruptly, she stepped away from him, taking his hand from her hair as she did. Her fingers caught for an instant in the bracelet at his wrist, twisting as she released him. At eye level the name engraved on the underside of the gold band leapt out at her.

Brett. A name that could belong to a man or a woman. But Nicole knew it could only be a woman.

A lover?

She was surprised at how much it hurt that there had been other women in his life. It was absurd to be so vulnerable and so naive. Jeb was a virile man, certainly far from ascetic. Two lives had changed since he'd been kind to a shy misfit. As she had assured Annabelle, he was her friend, no more. She'd had no claims on him then, and none now. Yet jealousy usurped anger.

Stepping briskly away, she turned her back on him. "We've wasted enough time with this. I have work to do."

She'd hoped he would take that as her final word, but Jeb had other ideas. He leaned against Annabelle's desk, propped one foot over the other and crossed his arms over his chest with the air of a man who'd settled in for the duration. Or until he got what he wanted.

"What do you have to do that's so pressing, Nicole?"

"This!" She waved a hand that encompassed the gallery. "This is what is so pressing. It's my livelihood. What I do."

"You can do it just as well Monday. Better, even, after you've taken some time off."

"Jeb..."

"It's a beautiful day."

"Beautiful days aren't unusual in Charleston."

"The water's calm, the wind is perfect."

"You said that."

Jeb ignored the caustic rejoinder. "Is there anything on the agenda for the rest of the day that Annabelle or your temporary help can't handle?"

"It isn't their gallery, they shouldn't have to handle the agenda."

"There's nothing," Annabelle chimed in for the first time. She had seen a masterful charmer at work, but Nicole wasn't cooperating. One look at the stiff, straight back told a story of a hard-fought battle. At the risk of having her head handed to her, and perhaps her severance pay, the chief assistant of the gallery decided to give one tiny nudge in the proper direction. "There's not much on tap for today, since this has been our slowest week on record."

"I know that, Annabelle." Nicole didn't spare her a glance.

"Then you know there's absolutely no reason you shouldn't accept Jeb's gracious invitation. A run down the coast may be exactly what you need."

"It isn't fair to ask you to cover for me again," Nicole said through her teeth.

"You aren't asking. I'm volunteering."

"There's Hunter's display to be done." Nicole was casting about for excuses.

"Which has you confounded, and which Ravenel can do with his eyes closed." Annabelle was reminding her, in not so subtle fashion, that in her current preoccupied state, she was less than useless. "Who knows, we might get something done around here if you weren't underfoot for a while."

"Underfoot!"

Jeb chuckled softly. "Sweetheart, I think you've just been thrown out of your own shop."

"But..."

"Hey." He straightened to his full height, and with a quick move he curled a hand about her arm. "You've been given a day off. A day you need, accept it gracefully."

"I don't need a day off." She sounded petulant even to herself, and she wondered who she was fighting, herself or Jeb. She wondered why.

"Yes, you do." There was laughter in his voice as he caught the scent of victory. "What better way to spend it than sailing with me?"

"What better way, indeed," Nicole murmured startling herself with abrupt capitulation. From the beginning she'd known there was nothing she'd wanted more than to go sailing with him. To feel the lazy rocking of the sea beneath her, and the sun on her skin. She wanted to learn more about Jeb, and a woman called Brett.

"Good girl." He tousled her hair as he had long ago, and grinned. "Say thank-you kindly to the nice lady, and go get your things. The *Gambler*'s in the harbor, ready and waiting."

"I don't have anything to wear sailing." Her look swept over the classic shantung. "This isn't quite the proper dress if I'm going to play at being an old salty."

"Not to worry." He tapped her on the nose, letting the pad of a finger trace the path of the scar. "I have some things on board that should fit."

Nicole wondered if these things so casually mentioned belonged to Brett.

"I hope you're hungry. There's a basket of food on board as well."

"The *Gambler*'s at harbor in Charleston, with clothing and food at the ready?" Nicole wrinkled her nose at him and the scar nearly disappeared. "You were pretty sure of me, weren't you?"

"Not on your life," Jeb declared. "I just didn't want to waste any time once I won the skirmish I knew I'd get."

He was arrogant, and too pleased with himself. If it were any other time, and any other man, Nicole would have taken great pleasure in popping that prideful bubble of masculine assurance. But not today. Not when she was feeling as giddy and happy as a child.

Spinning to Annabelle, she couldn't keep the smile from her face. "You're sure you don't mind?"

"I'm sure." Silver sounded, as if a thousand tiny bells, as Annabelle waved Nicole away. "Go! Have a perfect day. Rest, enjoy yourself. Dance by the fire."

Nicole caught her breath, exhaling in a long sigh. "Who knows?" she said with a thoughtful nod. "Maybe I will."

Jeb watched her go to the lounge. When the door closed behind her he turned back to Annabelle. He looked down at his fellow conspirator, who had kept silent through the entire encounter, until the last. "What's this about fire?"

"An enlightened suggestion."

Jeb waited, giving her ample opportunity to explain, but, judging by the set look on her face, he gathered he would wait forever. He'd been given all the explanation he was going to get. He knew when to cut his losses. "I should thank you."

"For what?" The question came quickly, bluntly.

"This is twice you've helped."

Annabelle leaned back in her chair. She was the rare person who was not intimidated to sit while another stood over her. Lacing her fingers, she leaned her chin on the steeple made of two. Through narrowed eyes she looked him up and down. He was a wolf, all right, and not a tame one. All the trappings of wealth and civilization couldn't change that. But untamed didn't mean unprincipled. She suspected Jeb Tanner was many things. Fierce? Without a doubt. Ruthless? Perhaps. Dangerous? Certainly. Deliberately cruel or malicious? Never.

She would stake all she held dear on it.

She *had* staked something very dear on it.

Her piercing stare finally settled on his face. Eyes as black as sin blazed up at him, searching, probing, seeking reason to believe or not to believe her gut instinct.

One long moment slipped into the next, and the next. Jeb held still for the brutal study. He knew what Annabelle was thinking. He knew why. He would do the same for a friend. But this was of far more import than mere friendship. Her decision would be critical, could mean success or failure for The Black Watch.

"All right," she said, as if the two of them had reached some unspoken covenant.

Jeb didn't respond. No response was needed. Her initial judgment would stand, but her guard was not down.

"Don't make this a mistake I'll regret." The rasp of steel rang in the muttered command. Annabelle Devereaux bore no resemblance to the comical femme fatale she played at.

With one more look filled with warning she turned her back on him, picked up her pen and began to write.

The cut off jeans were a bit long, and more than an inch or so too roomy at the waist. Nothing an extra cuff and an extra tug at the rope that served as a belt hadn't conquered. The matter of the faded T-shirt that reached nearly to her knees had been resolved by bunching it beneath her breasts and tying a bulky knot at her midriff.

With her legs stretched out before her, and a baseball cap pulled low over her forehead, she bore an uncanny resemblance to a castaway. But Jeb was certain there was never a castaway as striking as Nicole.

From his place at the wheel he kept her in his sight as she laughed and talked with Mitch and Matthew. With no effort at all, she'd captivated the men she thought were simply his crew. Even Matthew, who habitually held himself aloof, seemed at ease with her. There were no indications that troubling intuitions set him apart from her.

When she grew quiet, Matthew was last to leave her to drowse, replete and contented, in the sun as he joined Mitch below.

For the past hour the sloop had glided silently through channels and past small cays. The muted rustle and shuffle of men going about their chores was broken only by the sigh of the wind in the sails. Jeb reveled in the sound, in the surge of the sea beneath his feet, the buck of the wheel in his hand, the pleasant burn of the sun and wind at his back.

He was home. No matter what he did, no matter where, it would always be.

"Tired?" Matthew asked. As he touched Jeb's shoulder briefly, there was compassion in his eyes. Of two cultures, Apache and French, wild and urbane, with no common ground, he understood the toll of conflicting loyalties. He knew the need of choice, his own had been made. He was Apache now, his mother's heritage no longer existed for him. But he never forgot the agony of choosing, the shredded heart and soul. "Would you like me to take the wheel?"

Jeb shrugged aside his offer, but not ungraciously. He knew Matthew would understand. Matthew always understood.

The mast creaked, a sail snapped as the wind shifted. Matthew swayed easily with the plunge of the bow, a man of the desert at ease with his chosen loyalty. Keen eyes, as black as pitch, looked out over the sea then at Nicole. "She's sleeping."

Jeb nodded.

"You're wondering what I sense about her."

There was no need to answer or ask. Matthew was gifted with the virtually prescient power of his chosen people. He would explain in his own good time. Jeb listened to the wind, and waited.

"She's a gentle woman."

"Yes." Jeb's voice was gruff with disuse.

"Too gentle to be any part of what her brother has done."

"I know."

"I thought, perhaps, you did."

"What will she do when he comes?"

Matthew shook his head, the leather binding his long dark hair brushed his bare nape. A feather tangled with strands of turquoise beads. "I read people, my friend, and probabilities, not the future."

"Sorry."

Black eyes looked intently at Jeb. Bronze skin stretched tautly over expressionless features. "The critical question is what will you do?"

Jeb spun the wheel, adjusting course. The contentment of the sea was lost to him as Matthew called down the real world. "I'll do what I have to do, when the time comes."

No flicker of change showed on the Apache's face, but he knew what the words cost Jeb now. He feared what they would cost in the end. Just for a moment, he was tempted to tell him that the woman he loved, loved him as fiercely. But only for a moment.

Some things were better left for lovers to discover. And what better place than Eden?

"It's time you woke your lady for the first sighting of the island."

This time Jeb didn't shrug aside the offer. Stepping back he relinquished control on the sloop to Matthew. Treading from mid ship to the bow he bent over Nicole.

"Wake up, sweetheart," he said as he tipped the baseball cap from her eyes. "We've come to Eden."

Seven

Her first impression of the island, glimpsed as she roused from a restful sleep, was that it was unremarkable in that it was like so many other islands that dotted the coasts of the Carolinas and Georgia—low, lush, verdant and spectacularly beautiful. As the *Gambler* moved closer to shore, she saw her mistake. Eden was everything the barrier islands were, and more.

"How strange," she murmured as she tugged the brim of her cap lower to shield her eyes from the glare of the sun.

"The bluff?"

Nicole turned to Jeb. "I've never seen such an unusual elevation in the area."

"The rise is peculiar to Eden. And a good thing, too."

"How so?"

Jeb sidestepped her question. "It's a long story, too long for now. I'll tell you later, after we dock."

"Which we should be doing in about ten minutes," Mitch added to Jeb's comment as he stepped on deck. "Sit tight, Nick." He tossed a grin over his shoulder as he went to trim a sail. "Before you know it, you'll be in paradise."

"Paradise." It was easy to believe Eden lived up to its name. White sands, blue sky, bluer water and palmettos taller and thicker than any she'd ever seen. In its own way, the *Gambler* was paradise, as well. Maybe because she'd eaten with better appetite than she'd had in a while, and slept deeper than ever before. Or maybe it was the company of three courtly men, who seemed to have nothing better to do than see to her comfort.

"I missed my opportunity." Mitch lounged against the coaming, his task done for the time being.

"What opportunity?" she asked.

"To play pirate and shout 'land ho!' from the rigging."

"But I'm sure you have." Nicole laughed.

"Just once before." He grinned and waved expansively. "Here in this very corner of the sea, with the medicine man and Mitch, and a woman very much like you."

A woman very much like her.

Brett?

Had she sailed to Eden this same way? Felt as comfortable, as cared for. As safe?

Safe. That word again. A relative term. Arguable, when one looked, really looked, beyond the visage of her traveling companions. They were gallant to a fault, and courteous, but watchful and guarded. No move was unnecessary, no comment thoughtless. Even when they appeared totally relaxed, she sensed they were not. Nor would they ever be.

They spoke little to each other, yet communicated. A look spoke volumes, a subtle move even more.

At first she was sure she had imagined it, that it was simply the bond of excellent friends who'd worked and traveled together in close quarters for long intervals. By the time she recognized it as far more, she was too comfortable and too drowsy to care.

Wide awake, with the trill of excitement dancing through her, she sensed the same rapport, the watchfulness and guarded air that should have been illogical in an exercise as benign as approaching a deserted barrier island.

Yet it was there, no matter that they teased or played the gallant. The ambience of danger was strong, and with it the insinuation of potential violence balanced by unshakable

calm and poise. And all of it as natural to them as Mitch's
bent for teasing, or Matthew's reserved thoughtfulness and
Jeb's deep love of the sea.

Mitch Ryan, Matthew Sky, Jeb Tanner—quiet, consid-
erate men, who would be neither when the need came.

She didn't know how or why she knew these things. Only
that they were qualities so fierce, so exquisitely evolved, she
found herself questioning who these men were and what
they'd been before they became crew and captain of the
Gambler.

Perhaps, someday, she would know.

Jeb touched her arm, drawing her attention to starboard
as Matthew steered parallel with the island. "Watch," he
said with the throb of something she couldn't define in his
voice. "You'll only have a second."

Matthew slowed the engine to near idle, the sloop drifted
closer to shore. A sandbar visible in the pale, clear water
loomed at starboard, another at port. Neither Jeb nor Mitch
showed concern as Matthew threaded through as cleanly as
if they didn't exist.

"There." Jeb's hand tightened at her elbow, as he pointed
to thick undergrowth that crowded the edge of the sandy
beach. "Just past the palmetto bending to the sand."

They were moving slowly, the engine nearly soundless. At
first she saw only green. Thick, impenetrable green. Then it
seemed to fall away, a small clearing took shape, a flash of
space and openness beyond the occasional outcropping of
palmetto and sparse shrubs. As quickly, despite their slow
pace, it was gone.

Perplexed, she looked up at Jeb, not sure at all what she
was supposed to see, or had seen.

"You aren't dreaming or hallucinating. You saw a garden, and children. A girl and boy, part of a shrine."

"I assumed the island was deserted, most of the un-
charted isles are."

"Eden isn't inhabited at the moment, but it isn't deserted."

"A private retreat?"

Jeb nodded, as Matthew maneuvered the sloop toward a
dock tucked in a natural bay that notched the curving

shoreline. "Patrick McCallum bought it years ago for his wife, Jordana. There are other gardens now, but the one you saw was here before them. Beyond clearing away the worst of the underbrush, it was left as they found it, as it had been for nearly a century."

"I had no idea there was a place like this only an hour's sail from Kiawah. It's quite a pleasant surprise." The sloop scraped the padded dock, rocking in its own wake. Jeb's arms were there to hold her, before she could reach out for support.

"There are more surprises in store." His voice was deep, bass from the depths of his chest, vibrating against her back. "Eden is a sensualist's nirvana, as close as Patrick can come to the gift he most wants to give Jordana."

"Why not give her what he truly wants her to have?"

"Only a miracle can give her that." As Nicole leaned into him, her body swaying against his as the sloop bucked with the ebbing swells, there was a miracle of his own he would wish for.

"What miracle would that be?"

He drew her back against him, her body yielded to the pressure, fitting closely, perfectly, as if she were meant for him and him alone. His voice was rough, the effort to keep it even beyond him. "Her sight, Nicky."

"She's blind?"

"Yes," he said gently as he heard distress in her voice. "Jordana is blind."

"Dear heaven." Nicole closed her eyes, physically shutting out the bright shore, the brush, the water. But nothing could erase the mental image of Eden, of Patrick Mc-Callum's gift, a silver edged emerald in an azure sea. "How long?"

Jeb sensed what she was feeling, understood what she asked. "Jordana's never seen the island. She's been blind almost from birth."

"Then Patrick McCallum must be a very cruel man." To have this, to be a part of it and not share in it, not see it, would be a constant, painful reminder of Jordana's loss.

Jeb released her as Mitch leapt to the dock, securing the sloop with a coil of rope. "You're wrong. Patrick's a lot of things. Arrogant, stubborn, willful. No one could accuse him of being Mr. Congeniality, but he isn't cruel."

"I can't agree."

"You will." He took her hand. Eden waited. "Before the day is through, you'll understand."

The *Gambler* was a minute dot of rippling white. Watching it grow smaller and smaller, until it disappeared beyond the horizon, Nicole wondered all over again at the men who sailed it.

Matthew had come on shore but never strayed far from the sloop. Mitch, on the other hand, threw her a jaunty wave and disappeared into the interior of the island and didn't reappear for some time. Jeb played host leading her over carefully tended paths to a house of such natural and practical grandeur it left her speechless.

It wasn't until now, when the *Gambler* sailed from view, that she realized their arrival had been accomplished with all the carefulness of a friendly takeover. As if they expected nothing out of the ordinary, but wouldn't be caught unaware if there were.

Leaning on a balustrade, she looked out over gardens and shore and sea, and wondered again what manner of men were these.

"Surprised?" Jeb appeared at her side, a glass of ruby liquid in each hand.

Turning, she took the glass he offered. "A bit."

"Feeling stranded, cut off from the world?"

"Have you been reading my mind?"

He tucked her hair behind her ear, his fingers lingering at the fine line of her throat. "Just stating the obvious. It's a helpless feeling when your one connection with the outside world is beyond your reach."

He leaned on the balustrade beside her and, in spite of his observation, was more at ease than he'd been since they'd made shore. The island was clean. Mitch combed every inch of it with the aid of glasses from the single vantage on the bluff that offered a clear view of most of the terrain. Two stretches of shoreline were beyond his view. The north point and a small stretch of beach beyond the dock. The first had been visually searched as the *Gambler* moved close to the garden. The second, Matthew patrolled as he kept watch for any incoming vessels.

The house had been Jeb's assignment. He hadn't liked having Nicole with him as he went from room to room, under the guise of a tour. Still it was safest.

All was well. The *Gambler* sailed off the edge of the world, and for a few hours he had nothing to think of but Nicole.

For no reason but that he wanted to touch her, he let his fingers dance down her arm, bare beneath the pale green sleeve of the borrowed T-shirt. When she looked up at him, a question in eyes that reflected the color in deep, darkest jade, he smiled. "If it makes you feel any better, there's radio equipment in a shed at the back." Powerful, and in perfect working order, as reported by Mitch. "And a boat or two in dry dock on the channel."

"Doesn't surprise me," she observed dryly. "Considering the island, the house and everything in it and around it, a fleet wouldn't surprise me."

Jeb laughed. "That's something he hasn't thought of. Yet."

"Yet being the operative word, I think." Falling silent, she sipped her drink. Her arm tingled from shoulder to elbow long after his fingers moved away, but she didn't want to think of it, or why the slightest contact excited her. Drawing a long breath, she cast about for ways to put the thought from her. "This friend," she began, "the one that Mitch and Matthew had a sudden, burning need to visit, who is she?"

"Hattie Boone." He chuckled. "The experience of a lifetime. A unique woman who claims to be one-third white, one-third black, one-third bird and one-third fish."

"She must be unique if there are four thirds to the whole," Nicole observed drolly.

"She is, and she'd be first to tell you every inch of it is all woman."

"Maybe she should meet Annabelle, they have a lot in common."

"More than you know." He was thinking of a shared penchant for matchmaking, but before Nicole could ask what he meant he lifted his glass to the light. Ice and liquid sparkled like rubies. "If ever there was ambrosia, this is it. Hattie made it. It's never the same twice, never anything but delicious, and can never be found anywhere but here, on Eden. She's Patrick's itinerant caretaker and woman of all trades. Thanks to Hattie, and with her compliments, there's food in the cooler or the freezer when you're hungry."

"And fresh flowers on the table here on the deck," Nicole said, finishing for him. "She knew we were coming."

"Patrick called her to say we might."

"Now that we have, your crew has sailed away to visit with her."

"To know Hattie is to love her." Touching the rim of his glass to hers, he said, "Drink up, there's a lot I want to show you."

The day was too short, and Eden too beautiful. They'd begun, again, with the house, slower this time. Spacious, open, uncluttered, it brooked nothing that would trip a woman with eyes that could not see. Yet it was a house of textures. Smooth and rough, delicate and sturdy, wicker and bamboo, mahogany and teak. Coarse silks, sculpted brocades, burlap, gossamer and homespun. The list was luxuriant and endless.

A feast to the touch.

For Jordana.

Nicole had begun to understand Patrick's gift, to appreciate it, when Jeb led her through gardens rich with the scent of roses, lilies, oleander and lowly beach daisies. At their borders the path turned rugged and difficult. Vines coiled over it as it deteriorated into a meandering trail. Twisted limbs and fallen trees threatened to block their way, low hanging Spanish moss brushed faces and shoulders. After fifteen minutes of rough going, what seemed an impenetrable wall loomed before them, then moved beneath Jeb's hand like magic.

The gate swung open, dragging cloistering vine and ivy with it, into a garden nearly as unkempt as the path. The clearing was small, and crowded with ferns, and more ivy and banks of wild roses. In the center stood the figures she'd glimpsed from the sloop. A young girl shared booty from the sea with a wide-eyed lad. But it was carved of stone, green with age, not cast in bronze as she had thought.

"Of all the island, of all Patrick has created for her, this is Jordana's favorite," Jeb told her as she stared in bewilderment.

Nicole thought of the paths she'd trod, the house, the gardens. Each of them carefully planned, so that a woman attuned to her senses could wander them independently.

It would be precious independence. And the greatest gift of all.

But not offered here in a cherished place. Only an hour ago she would've been quick to judge, and judge harshly, what seemed a cruelly thoughtless act heaped upon a cruel condition. But she'd learned that nothing was as it seemed on Eden.

"Tell me," she said as she sank to the small bench at the edge of the clearing. "I'd like to know about this place."

Jeb nodded and sat beside her. Taking her hand in his, he looked about the garden. At the wild flowers, the gnarled live oaks and magnolias threaded through with curling vines. "One of the past owners of the island was Jeremiah Brody. He made the garden for his children who were lost at sea. It had fallen into thorny disorder when Patrick came here. Because Jordana wanted it left as they'd found it, he did only minimal restorative work. She wanted it kept as a secret garden, the sort the children would have loved."

His fingers laced through hers, his thumb stroked the pulse at her wrist. A breeze from the sea set magnolias and oaks and palmettos rustling, each with a timbre of their own.

"Some think of it as a sorrowful place. But Jordana says no," he resumed in reverent tones. "Listen. It's only the wind in the trees, but Jordana's certain she hears the laughter of children mingled in it."

"She's fond of children?"

"Enough to make them her life's work. She gives her time and uses her talent with the guitar to help children like herself understand that nothing is beyond them."

The garden was more than a favorite place. Much more. Every sense was alive, keening, receptive. Nothing was beyond Jordana here, for one didn't need sight to feel the peaceful mood. For the first time, Nicole believed. "She truly does love this place."

"Better than any other part of the island."

Nicole considered the carefully groomed paths through the other gardens and to the beach. Not one was anything but perfect. No roots cropped unexpectedly from the ground, no low hanging limbs dipped into the path threatening to scratch or claw. While the path to Jeremiah Brody's garden was nearly impassable. "She loves it best, but she can't come here alone."

"She doesn't want to. For Jordana this is a place to be shared with Patrick."

Nicole looked down at their joined hands. The bracelet glinted about his wrist. Had he brought Brett here? Had she listened as raptly to his story of Jordana and Patrick? Had she felt heartsick and ashamed for envying a truly rare and abiding love?

"Hey." Jeb's fingers skimmed along her jaw, lifting her face. "What's this? Have you forgotten already?"

"Forgotten?"

"That this is a happy place. Long faces aren't allowed."

Nicole stared up at him, her mind reeling at the tenderness she saw. Brett didn't matter, nothing mattered except the feel of his hand at her throat and the look in his eyes. "I haven't forgotten."

"Then where's my smile? Gotta have it, you know, or I'll think you don't like my surprise."

"I like it." A slow smile, straight from her heart, spread across her face. "I like everything about Eden."

"That's my girl." Then he kissed her, a simple brushing of his mouth against hers, but enough to send tremors rushing through him. He'd known that her mouth would be soft and, when she got past the first surprise, yielding. What he didn't expect was the flash of need and desire that was nearly his undoing. He'd wanted her before, but never quite like this.

Drawing away while he still could, his breath coming in hard deep gasps, he tried to smile. "Jordana says this place is magic."

Nicole didn't answer, she had no words. She'd been kissed, but not like Jeb kissed her. Never like Jeb kissed her. The shock of all the nameless needs he stirred in her left her confused, a little afraid, and desperate for more.

The wind whirled through the garden, the rustle of leaves rose to a chortle. Jeb closed his eyes, hearing the laughter of children, recalling, deliberately, the one addition Jordana had made to the garden. A stone buried at the children's feet, covered now with ivy. But he didn't need to see to remember the words carved in slanting script.

Where There's Laughter There Must Be Peace And Truth, And No One Can Be Sad Or Frightened.

Truth.

Jeb Tanner, retired stockbroker extraordinaire, was anything but the truth.

He'd been angry with Simon for sullying Eden again with the troubles of The Black Watch. Now he saw himself as the greatest offender of all.

"Enough." Scooping up the cap his kiss had tumbled from her head, he shot to his feet, a curse under his labored breath, reviling his thoughts, himself. In his anger, he had presence of mind enough to see the bewilderment in her eyes. And he hated himself more.

"Sorry." He wrapped a hand around her cheek. "I didn't mean to startle you." Pretending to misunderstand was easier for both of them. "I just remembered something I promised to do for Patrick."

"Then I shouldn't delay you." She needed a moment to regain her composure, and to discover if she were glad or sorry he backed away. "Go on and I'll be along later."

He hadn't sunk quite low enough to lead a woman into a virtual wilderness, then leave her. He wasn't quite that angry or that desperate.

"We came together, Nicky. We'll go back the same way." He didn't hear the harsh note in his voice, nor see her flinch

as he took her hand again to lift her to her feet. "If you'd
like, you can spend time on the beach while I do what I need
to do. Jordana has some extra swimsuits at the pool house.
They might be a bit roomy, but should suffice. If you tire of
walking, or get too much sun, there's a cabana on the South
beach."

He sounded like a tour guide. Cold-eyed, bored, hand-
ing out information in a monotone. Nicole looked away,
grasping at his suggestion. "I think I'd like to walk for a
while on the beach."

"The suits—"

"I don't need a suit."

"As you wish."

He led her back to the main grounds. Retracing their steps
as carefully as before, he kept tree limbs from her face, moss
from her hair, touching her only when he had to, releasing
her quickly each time. As if the feel of her skin was abhor-
rent.

At the path leading to the South beach, he handed her the
cap, muttered a terse, unintelligible comment that might
have been goodbye, take care, or go to hell, and strode away
to a small building behind the main house.

Nicole scuffed her bare toes in the sand. A broken sand
dollar tumbled to the edge of the surf, scattering tiny bits of
its center over the sand. There was a legend about those gull-
shaped pieces, but she couldn't recall it. She didn't try. After all, there were legends about everything, weren't there?

Charleston had more legends than one could remember,
Kiawah had Folly's Castle, Eden had the children's garden.
Who knew? Perhaps one day there would be a legend of an
idiot woman who pined away...

She stopped, staring blankly at the shell. "For what?" A
memory, a dream, out of confusion? All of the above?

"Like a fool."

Jeb had kissed her, and each time it rocked her to the
depths of heart and soul. But what had it meant to him?
Was his interest in her simply the natural condition of a
stranger in a strange land gravitating to an old friend? Or
was it more?

Frustrated, she spun in place and back again, wondering where to go, what to do. On one hand, she could stand here all day playing twenty questions when she didn't have twenty answers. On the other, she could enjoy a rare holiday in a rare place. Common sense opted for the latter.

"Smart cookie," she muttered. Now if her mind would only listen to reason. Doggedly she set out to walk away her troubles. Walk them right into the sand, she would.

Thirty-seven-and-one-half minutes later, as she glanced at her watch out of habit, she realized she'd done exactly that. Or, at least, had put them into perspective.

"Wisdom sometimes walks on bare feet," she misquoted the adage shamelessly. Her mother, who had been old enough to be her grandmother, and given to salving what she considered life's little problems with endless proverbs, would be proud.

Always a Band-Aid when she needed a bandage, but she'd learned to hold on to her pride and make the best of what she was given.

For a while Tony had given her more. And then Jeb.

"Jeb."

She scuffed the sand again, and knew her barefoot wisdom was for naught. She was as guilty as her mother, a Band-Aid for a bandage, a temporary measure for a permanent condition.

"I love Jeb Tanner. I *have* loved Jeb Tanner since I was fifteen. I *will* love Jeb Tanner until the day I die."

There, dammit! She'd dreamed it, thought it, felt it, at last she'd said it.

"I love him," she said again, whispering when she wanted to shout, knowing she never could, and accepting it.

A playful breeze kissed her cheek and caught the words, as if it shared her secret and would keep it. Nicole smiled a sad smile and wondered if Eden offered an invisible shoulder to cry on.

But she wouldn't cry, not even for Jeb. She'd finished with her tears for him a long time ago. But she hadn't finished with him. Not by a long shot. He'd begun by seeing her as 'the kid' and ended by seeing the woman. He wanted her, and he was fighting it.

"He's going to lose. I'm going to see to it." Tossing her cap to the beach, she tilted her chin, letting the breeze ruffle her hair. "My gift, to me," she murmured. "From Eden."

Jeb found her later, sitting in the sand, staring at the sea.

"All done?" she asked without looking away from some distant point.

"What?" He frowned down at her, her hat was gone, her nose was sunburned. "Done with what?"

"The favor." She looked up at him. "The one you promised Patrick."

"Yeah." He swallowed and nodded. "All done."

Busy work. He'd worked like hell, and all it had been was busy work.

"I think Patrick's lucky to have a friend like you."

"Maybe." In the flush of the sun, her eyes were greener than he'd ever seen them. He flexed his fingers, wanting to touch her cheek, feel the heat. "I...ah." He looked away. The sea was as calm as a lake, an irresistible invitation. "Would you like to go for a swim?"

"No." Swimming meant two choices, skinny-dipping or accepting a suit from Jordana's closet. He'd assured her no one would mind. He was dead wrong. Someone minded all right. Nicole Callison minded. She was already wearing one stranger's clothes, a second would be too much.

"Tell me about Brett."

"What?" For Jeb the question came out of nowhere and left him totally perplexed.

Nicole climbed to her feet; dusting sand from her hands, she grasped his wrist, lifting it until the bracelet glinted in the sun. "Tell me about Brett."

"How do you know about Brett?"

She gestured to the gold band lying against his tanned arm. "This, and later Mitch."

Jeb remembered. "When he went through that nonsense about playing pirate, crying 'land ho' from the rigging."

"He said she was a woman much like me."

"She is." He offered nothing else, asking instead, "What more would you like to know?"

What did she want to know? That Brett was wonderful and exciting? Special to Jeb? Didn't she know that already? Wasn't the bracelet proof of it? "I don't want to know anything. It's none of my business. Forget I asked."

She turned away, anxious to put space between them.

"What the hell?" Jeb caught her arm, spinning her around. "What's the matter with you?"

"What's the matter?" Her voice was low, a whisper barely heard above the wash of the surf. "You know as well as I do." Her breasts heaved beneath the clinging T-shirt. "Damn you, Jeb Tanner, you know. I've loved three men in my life. My father, my brother and you. One day you walked out of my life without a backward glance. Three years later Tony did the same. I never heard from him again. Not a word. Not even when our parents died. I lost a friend, I lost a brother and one by one, my parents. It took a while, but finally I put all the heartache behind me.

"Then one day you walked into my gallery and back into my life. And it began again."

"What began again, Nicole?" His throat was dry, his heart pounded in every sinew and nerve.

"Do you want the words? Do you need them?"

"Yes." The admission was a growl, guttural, harsh. "With every dotted *i* and crossed *t*."

"*Desire,*" she flung at him. "There's your dotted *i*. *Want,* a crossed *t*. *Need,* thrown in just for the hell of it. Yes, I was fifteen and too young. But I'm not fifteen, anymore, not by a long shot. There." She jerked her arm from his hold. "Are you satisfied? Is that enough?"

As the force of her violent move backed her away, he went with her. Advancing one small step at a time. He'd fought himself, he'd fought for honor and integrity. But he couldn't fight Nicole. Not when she stood before him, a magnificent woman, throwing down a gauntlet no man could refuse. "No, it isn't enough."

"Then what more do you want?"

"This." His hand flashed out, catching in her hair, yanking her roughly to him. "I want this," he muttered as his head dipped to hers. "I want you."

His mouth closed over hers, hard and demanding, with all the pent-up passion he'd fought. He didn't know what he expected, or if he expected anything at all, but when her mouth opened beneath his, responding with passion for passion, it rocked him to the very core. If he'd thought to stop with a punishing kiss, the thought was lost.

As he tore his lips away, lifting his head, searching for a place, he knew nothing on earth would stop him from making love to her here, now. On Eden. In the sand if there was nowhere else.

The cabana. It stood at his back, he'd nearly forgotten it. Sweeping her from her feet, he held her close to his chest. Sand flew as he spun around. He wondered vaguely what he was doing, then Nicole sighed and kissed the sensitive flesh at the side of his neck as she buried her face in his shoulder.

Then he didn't think at all.

The cabana was only a shanty with four corner posts and a thatched roof over beach sand. A crude and tiny square of shade and cool, but enough. One kick sent a bench tumbling from his way. Setting her on her feet, he kissed her again, and her mouth was enough to drive him mad, if he weren't already there.

His shirt drifted to the sand, and he lost his breath as her palm stroked over his chest. His fingers were clumsy with the knot at her breasts. The twisted knot gave an inch, then uncoiled. His rasping curse turned to a prayer as the shirt floated to join his, and her breasts were free for him to caress and to kiss.

"Nicole," he whispered as he bent to take a taut nipple in his mouth.

Dazed with wonder, she gave herself to pleasure she'd never known. But soon, as her hands moved over his bare back, as his tongue curled and tugged at her breasts, it wasn't enough. She wanted more. She needed more.

"Jeb."

Only his name.

Lifting his mouth from her breast, he looked deeply into her eyes. Desire mirrored desire. She ached for him, for all of him, as much as he ached for her.

"It isn't enough," he whispered cryptically. "But with you, will it ever be?"

There was no time to ponder what he meant, no time to care, as he drew her down to a careless bed made of discarded clothing. Grasping her wrists, pinning them to the ground at each side of her head, he rose over her. For a long, slow moment he looked again into her eyes. There was fire in them, emerald fire, as his mouth moved over her face and breasts, but he wanted a conflagration. He wanted the untamed passion, he wanted the madness, the need, the hurt, the sweet pain. He wanted her to writhe with it, and cry out. He wanted her to tremble with wanting, as he trembled.

And even then, it wouldn't be enough.

"Jeb." She strained to his kiss, never sure if it would fall on her breasts, an aching nipple, or the hollow of her navel. Never really sure that she would survive the next onslaught, but certain she would die without it.

Her head thrashed to and fro. She fought against his pinioning hold. She wanted to touch him, caress him, drive him to the brink. She wanted more. She wanted everything.

"Jeb!"

"Yes." He moved over her, his lips brushing hers in a long languid kiss, as his body joined gently with hers. Then gentleness was beyond him.

Every tortuous pleasure he wanted for her she gave to him. Their bodies merged, then merged again, and again, and again. Hotter, wilder, demanding and giving. Spiraling down and down into the pulsing darkness of release.

"Nicky! My sweet Nicky," he cried on a shuddering breath.

Her own cries answered.

Then the world was still.

Jeb braced an arm on a corner post of the cabana as a minuscule patch of white drifting in the ocean became a sail. The *Gambler* would be docking in less than an hour.

He hadn't bothered to dress. It was a little late for modesty, and common sense and honesty. It was late for everything. But he could explain. "You asked about Brett."

Nicole paused in the act of looping the rope at her waist. She looked at his straight, unyielding back, at the bracelet. "It doesn't matter. It's none of my business."

"She's a friend, a good friend," he continued as if she hadn't spoken. "The bracelet is a token of thanks. If you read the entire inscription, you'd see."

"Fine." She bent to gather her shirt from the sand.

"Matthew and Mitch have one exactly like it." So did Simon, but it wasn't necessary to bring someone she didn't know into this.

"Why?"

"The way she figures it, the man she loves, her husband now, is alive because of us."

"Is it true?"

"Maybe." He shrugged. "There was trouble here, they hid on the bluff, then put out to sea. They'd been drifting for a day when we found them. Jamie had a shattered hand and was delirious. They might have survived long enough to make it to shore."

"But they might not have."

He shrugged again. "Who knows."

They were only the sparsest facts of a much larger story, but intuition told her she wouldn't hear any more. Shouldn't. "Then I'm glad you could help."

"Yeah." He turned then. Magnificently male, and heartbreakingly sad. "The sloop will be docking within the hour. We need to get away before darkfall. If you'd like to take a shower, wash away the sand, there are six bathrooms in the house." Collecting his rumpled clothes, he didn't look at her. "Use any one you like."

"All right," she said, but he was striding away, and still without a backward look.

Nicole sat in gathering shadows; hands folded to still their restlessness, she looked up at the portrait of Jordana. A special woman, a special place.

"Thank you for sharing your Eden," she whispered. "I'll never forget."

Rising, she went to the door. The scent of flowers drifted to her. With a steady hand she reached out to pluck a wild rose from a vase. A memento.

Just like that, it was done. As she stepped through the door, closing it behind her, her day on Eden was ended. She had run an emotional gamut here—from elation to despair—as passion was spent and madness returned to reason, with not one tender word.

The moon was rising, the waiting sloop gleamed in its early light. As she took one last look about her, there were no regrets for the bargain she'd made with herself.

As long as she lived, she would never regret loving Jeb.

Eight

—

"**A**nnabelle!" Nicole stopped abruptly as the bell over the gallery door jangled her nerves. If she were as tall as Jeb, she could stop the chiming on one note. But she wasn't as tall as Jeb, and she didn't intend to spend the day mooning about him.

"Good morning." A dark look flashed at her. "Although, for the life of me, I can't find anything good about it."

"You're early." Nicole went to her desk, depositing an arm load of mail she'd picked up from the post office. Annabelle was almost never temperamental, but when she was, it was best to leave her alone to work through her mood.

"Ahh, an intelligent perception from an intelligent woman."

Nicole looked up from the stack of letters she was sorting, astonished at the bitter sarcasm. "Annabelle, are you upset with me?"

"Of course I'm not upset with you. Why should I be?"

"I did leave you in charge here while I went out to play, when I shouldn't have."

"And why shouldn't you? What's wrong with the idea that you should grab a little happiness and excitement, if you wish? Goodness knows, you've worked hard enough and long enough without it. Anyone would think you were supposed to be a monk, or something."

"Nun," Nicole corrected automatically.

"All right, nun."

Dropping the letters, Nicole laid her hands, palms down, on the desk. "I think you'd better tell me why you're so angry."

Annabelle sighed and slumped down into the chair at her own station. "I'm not upset with you, Nicole. But I am angry, in fact, I'm more than angry. I'm mad as hell with Mrs. Atherton, and Ashley and, most of all, myself."

Nicole leaned back and closed her eyes. "Let me guess. Mrs. Atherton has been gossiping." Hardly a guess, she should have known it was coming.

"Second to harassing us for ridiculous prices, isn't it what she does best?"

"What is it this time? Jeb?"

"Bingo! She saw you leave the marina with him. Fueled by what she witnessed the day he arrived in Charleston, it was enough cloth to make a whole garment of speculations. Stated loud and long, of course. And you *don't* want to hear what they are."

"I can imagine, that's more than enough," Nicole muttered. A twinge of pain settled in her temple. She brushed at it with an impatient hand, as if she would brush it away. But it wouldn't go away. None of it would. "So, Mrs. Atherton has sharpened her spiteful tongue. That isn't new. But why Ashley? Why are you angry with him? And yourself?"

"He was here when the old biddy did some reconnaissance. A fact-finding raid, actually, to add to her tale. Once she embroidered on them, of course."

"Why was Ashley here?"

"He had a new watercolor. A drawing of Folly's ruin at sunrise." Annabelle tilted her head like a curious bird. "With all of Charleston to choose from, why would he draw the ruin?"

"He heard what Mrs. Atherton had to say?" Nicole was more concerned with Ashley's state of mind than his drawing.

"Every lurid speculation, until I invited her to leave."

"Good."

"What came next was not so good. Ashley had a tantrum, and being the smart woman I am, I scolded him, and lectured him about life, and that you needed to have one of your own. And that Mrs. Atherton had no right to judge. The poor man probably understood only every third word, but some of my message got across. He kept thumping his chest and saying, 'me, me, me.' Then there was something about kisses and best."

"How did you calm him down?"

"I didn't. He tore up the drawing of the ruin, then he smashed the paintings he did at the zoo, and ran away. I could swear he was crying." Annabelle's face was haggard, her eyes shone with stifled tears. "Have you ever kicked a puppy?"

"No." Nicole looked to the exhibit wall. Order had been restored, but the paintings that hung over Hunter Slade's small sculptures were not Ashley's. She buried her face in her hands. The twinge was an avalanche. "No." She sighed sadly and looked at Annabelle. "But I know exactly how you feel."

"How could you?"

"Because this is all my fault." Ashley had drawn the ruin because it was a rare, unthreatening place for him.

Annabelle snorted indelicately. "How could anything be your fault when you were off sailing on the mighty ocean blue?"

"It's my fault because there's more to the incident in the park than you know." Once she'd begun, the rest of the story spilled out. She left nothing out, spared herself nothing as she described Jeb kissing her, she kissing him back. Ashley afraid and crying for her. Then, finally, the morning at the ruin, Ashley's anger and rivalry with Jeb. "I tried to assure him. To be honest, I can't remember now exactly what I said. I don't know if I put the idea I liked him best in his head, or if Jeb did. Maybe Ashley settled on the idea himself. I just don't remember.

"But who or how isn't important, anymore. The damage was done the minute I stepped on the *Gambler*. Ashley painted the ruin because he was happy there. I doubt he ever will be again. He has no idea what the word betray means, but, thanks to me, he knows how it feels."

"You didn't do this." Annabelle's eyes were hard. "The old biddy did." An angry gesture indicated strongly that if the old biddy were here now, she should stand in fear of being throttled.

"Perhaps she was the messenger, but I was the catalyst." Nicole's gaze moved over newly hung paintings. They were excellent, but not as compelling as what Ashley had done. "Where is he now?"

Annabelle was silent for so long, Nicole turned to her. "Annabelle?"

"That's the worst of it. Nobody knows where he is. I looked for hours. Harry looked for hours." Her shoulders moved in an expression beyond defeat. "Nothing. Not a trace. I even considered calling in the city police, but that would only make matters worse. Ashley is petrified of uniforms."

He had been since his childhood, when uniformed officials had taken him from his beloved streets and locked him in a cage. Nicole knew because, in his few and halting words, Ashley had told her. Only a few words were needed to express his fear, and the hurt, that the people he had trusted had betrayed him. Now she'd added herself to that long, terrible list.

"I know him better than anyone. Maybe I can find him."

"Don't be ridiculous, Nicole. If Harry Devereaux couldn't find him... Nicole! Nicole!"

The bell chimed, the door closed, and Annabelle had the gallery all to herself.

There were customers when Nicole returned. Lunch-break browsers, who looked but seldom bought. Out of principle, and because she would have it no other way, they were given full attention.

Annabelle was at her desk, dealing with three people simultaneously. One was actually buying, one needed directions, one simply wanted attention. Slanting her an apologetic look, Nicole hurried to the lounge, she was in no condition to deal with customers. Her blouse was soiled, the hem of her skirt had ripped loose. A long angry scratch scored her cheek from the bridge of her nose to her ear. Her frame of mind was worse.

For once, Annabelle tapped on the door first, and then barged in. "Good Lord! You look awful."

"Thanks a bunch."

"You didn't find him."

"I went everywhere. Every one of his favorite places. I saw signs that he'd been there, but who knows when? His regular customers say he hasn't been at the hotel lobby to shine their shoes in days."

"What are you going to do?"

"I wish I knew what to do. You saw him, Annabelle, do you think there will be trouble?"

"Only as much trouble as a pouting three-year-old can cause."

"A big three-year-old."

"Yes, well, there is that." Annabelle came to sit beside her, taking away the damp cloth she held to her cheek. "Oh, wow! Maybe you'd better get this treated."

"It's just a scratch."

"Then you're really okay?"

"I'm fine, Annabelle." She took back the cloth and pressed it to her cheek. Out of sight was not quite out of mind, she could see it in her friend's face. Gently she assured her, "It's nothing, really."

"It's a lot more than that and you know it, but I won't nag. Instead, I'd better get back to the gallery. I herded the gawkers out, and put a sign on the door saying I'd be back in fifteen minutes. All we need now is for Mrs. Atherton to see it."

"More gossip."

"Without question. But, tell me, what does it matter now?"

"It doesn't to me, I just hope that Jeb won't..." She snapped her fingers. The bleak look eased from her features. "That's it."

"That's what?" Annabelle demanded. "You aren't making sense."

"Yes I am, for the first time today. Jeb, Annabelle."

"What about him?"

"He can find Ashley. Or, if he can't, his crew can."

"The men out of *GQ?*"

"Precisely." Nicole opened a drawer; taking out a soft bound book, she turned through it searching for the number she needed.

"They're sailors, remember. Not Indian scouts."

"That's where you're wrong. Matthew Sky may not be a scout, but he's part Indian. Part, only by blood. His heart is pure Apache."

There were no numbers listed for Jeb Tanner. Information proved to be a recording, informing Nicole in a tinny voice the number was unlisted and unpublished and not available. Dropping the receiver in its cradle, she gathered up her purse. "Close up for the day, Annabelle. It will be simpler than answering a lot of questions."

"Wait. Where are you going this time?"

"I'm going to Kiawah." Nicole paused in the open doorway. "To find Jeb."

"What the devil?" Jeb stood on his deck, glaring at her. The glass he held nearly slid from his fingers.

"I need to talk to you." Ignoring his shock, Nicole dodged past him, going into the great room without an invitation.

"You're mighty right you do." Jeb followed, set the glass aside and took her face in his hands. "Good God! What happened?"

She tried to turn away, he wouldn't let her. "It's nothing."

"Nothing, hell." He tilted her cheek to the light and grimaced. "What son of a bitch did this to you? Tell me."

"Nobody did it, Jeb." She laid her hands on his chest, a placating motion. "I did it myself on a shrub."

"How?" he snarled. "Why?"

"I was looking for Ashley."

"Why?" Anger seethed in him, a muscle rippled in his jaw as his teeth clenched on the question.

"Jeb, Ashley is—"

"Forget it. I don't want to hear it. Not yet."

"But—"

"First things first." His hands were heavy on her shoulders as he propelled her down a hall to his bedroom. When surprise registered on her face as he pushed her down on the bed, he snapped, "Just sit there and don't worry, sweetheart. I brought you here to do something about your face, not make love to you. Though, God help me, I've thought of it often enough since Saturday."

By the time her world righted itself again, he was rummaging through a medicine cabinet. Listening to a steady stream of snarled curses, some she'd never heard before, she folded her hands primly in her lap and wondered what to expect next from this mercurial man who seemed to be two men in one.

One made love to her, fiercely. With a touch and a kiss, he suspended time and tide. He was her world, and, for that little while on Eden, she'd thought she was his. The words he'd whispered were tender, intimate, so sweet she'd wanted him again and again.

Anything so right had to be shared. He had to feel as she did. She was sure of it, until he'd walked away without a backward look.

The trip back from Eden had been strained. Jeb had kept his distance, as if he were angry with her. Mitch had tried to fill the empty silences with his teasing at first. Then even he'd given up. Matthew had spoken only once, touching her shoulder, smiling a bittersweet smile as if he knew what she felt, murmuring a single word—"Patience."

What should patience have to do with loving?

She didn't understand then, she didn't understand now. Especially after encountering this other Jeb. The one who, after nearly two days of ignoring her, was fussing over a dirty blouse and torn skirt as if it were a calamity. From his alarm one would think the mark on her face was a matter of life or death. That was a new one, a life-threatening scratch.

"When the hell did you do this?" He was standing over her, furious and fierce, enunciating each word as if he were having trouble with his voice. Then he knelt at her feet, a pan filled with a disinfectant solution at his knee, and sundry salves and bandages in a box. "What fool let you go wandering around in scrub and whatever?"

"Ouch!" She shied away from the sudden, odorous sting of Betadine.

"Be still."

"I will not be still." Grasping his wrist, she took his hand from her face. "To back up and answer your question about this—this mortal wound, I just did it not more than an hour ago. And as to the fool who let me wander around in the 'scrub or whatever,' as you call it, the answer is nobody *lets* me do anything. *I* did this to myself, and I'll survive without anyone fussing over me like a mother hen."

"I'll fuss when I damn well please, and however I please."

"Jeb, stop. Please!" She looked into his heated stare. "What are we doing? I came to ask for help finding Ashley, not to fight with you."

"Find Ashley? Is that how you got this? Running all over looking for some idiot—" When he realized what he'd said, he drew a deep breath and closed his eyes as he sank back on his heels. "Ahh, no." His sigh was long, and heavy with regret. "Obviously if there's an idiot here, his name is Jeb Tanner, not Ashley."

Climbing to his feet, he went to the window, keeping his back to her. "I'm sorry. I don't know what got into me. Maybe it was the thought that your face would be scarred."

"It wouldn't be the first, or have you forgotten?"

"I haven't forgotten." He would never forget pulling her from the water, half conscious and bleeding profusely after a surfboard hit her squarely in the face. It was the first time he'd noticed Tony's reaction was wrong. He'd been impassive, a clinical observer, not a worried brother. Jeb worried enough for both of them, especially when she insisted on going back into the water. To please her brother, because he expected it. "You fought me then, even when you were reeling and too dizzy to stand."

"I don't want to fight you now," she said quietly. "And if I seem ungrateful, I'm not. I appreciate that you care."

He faced her, his gaze moving over her feverishly. He'd told himself he needed distance. But there could never be enough distance to put her out of his mind. To keep from wanting her. To stop the ache that lived inside him. "Are you all right?"

She opened her mouth to respond, then shut it tight as she realized he wasn't speaking of a scratch on her face. "I'm all right," she said after a while. It wasn't really a lie, nor the truth, but she was getting there. "I'll be fine."

"I didn't mean to hurt you."

"I know."

"No." He shook his head. "You have no idea."

Nicole's chin lifted, her eyes glittered. "Are you sorry you made love to me, Jeb?"

"Yes." The word was a hiss. An agitated hand raked through his hair, tugging at it viciously. "No!"

"Which is it, Jeb? Yes, or no?" She didn't blink, didn't move. Had she been a fool? She could stand anything but that.

"Nicky..."

"Yes, or no?"

He muttered a low oath, a word that was becoming too familiar. "There's a lot I regret, and even more that I should. Making love to you should be one of them. I should carry it on my soul like a brand, but I'm not sorry." Even a liar and a rogue couldn't regret his one small taste of heaven. "God forgive me, I'm not."

The blow she feared hadn't fallen. The defensive posture of her body eased, the band constricting her heart snapped. "Then that's all that matters."

"There can't be any more than that, Nicky. Some day you'll understand why." And on that day, she would hate him.

She left the bed to go to him. Standing before him, she laid her fist over his heart. The beat of it was strong, as he was strong. As she must be. When she bargained with herself, it was to have what little she could. With no regrets. "I'm not asking for any more."

"You deserve better."

"Then what I deserve and what I want are totally different."

"Sweetheart, I wish..." But she never heard what he wished. Instead, he drew her to him, burying his face in her hair. He held her close until the tension drained from him, and every taut muscle uncoiled. Lifting her face with a finger under her chin, he kissed her cheek beneath the scratch, he kissed her eyes. As she looked up at him, trusting him, he murmured again. "I wish."

When his lips brushed hers, his kiss was exquisite, poignant, rocking her world beneath her feet. As her mouth yielded to his, tears she couldn't shed for a man who seemed lost and lonely glittered in her eyes.

Slowly, he put her from him and lifted a hand. "Peace?"

Nicole smiled, a smile too brilliant, and put her hand in his. "Peace."

"Tell me again what he said." Matthew leaned forward, his arms resting on the desk, his hands loose, relaxed. Before Annabelle could object, he added, "I know you've told me until you're sick of telling me, but, please, just once more."

Arms folded, face twisted in deep study, Annabelle drifted through the gallery, moving abstractedly from print to painting, bronze to stone, trailing her fingers over each frame and figure lightly. At the newest display, that had once belonged to Ashley, she stopped, focused, racked her memory.

The gallery had closed for the day as Nicole suggested, and the showroom was quiet now, eerily quiet. Other than her interrogator, only Jeb and Nicole were present. Neither of them moved or spoke, but she felt the weight of hopeful stares.

"Look!" She whirled about to Matthew. "This is a waste of time. I've told you all I know. Wouldn't you do better to be out there, going to Ashley's old haunts? His favorite places, before he does something foolish?"

Matthew accepted her anger placidly. No expression showed on his lean, hard face. His black eyes were unwavering, but not unkind. Annabelle's guilt-laden irritation and frustration sparked in the air like an electric current, but he offered no appeasing remarks, no false apology for his incessant prodding.

Expecting contradiction, needing it to fuel her frustration, Annabelle faltered, her criticism fading like ripples from a stone thrown in a pond.

Matthew sat motionless and might have seemed cast of bronze or carved of stone, were it not for the slight rise of his chest with each slow, shallow breath. He was patient, a watcher, like his chosen people. In the muted light, with shadows falling over his features, the trappings of modern dress were not at odds with the inherent traits of his lineage. Nor with the flash of feather and stone on the band he wore at his nape, an alternative to the traditional headband.

Fierce pride of the *N'de,* the Apache, was reflected in his bearing, their restrained strength in his stillness. Intelligence and wisdom, and something beyond shone in his dark, slanting gaze.

Matthew Winter Sky would be an implacable enemy, but faithful beyond measure in friendship. It was the latter that commanded Annabelle's compliance when he said simply, "Please."

"All right." Though she tried to cling to the farce of her anger, there was no heat in her reply. Carefully, as she had before, she recounted Ashley's arrival at the gallery. His proud offering of the newest painting, his disappointment that Nicole was away for the day. "That's when the old biddy came bursting in. A vulture riding hell for leather, bearing tales, looking for more. When she saw it upset Ashley that Nicole had gone sailing with Jeb, she made it sound as bad as possible."

An apologetic glance at Nicole's pale face halted her recitation. Then squaring her shoulders she addressed Matthew again. "Repeating what she proposed and surmised won't find Ashley, so we'll forget that part."

"You showed her the door," Matthew prompted, adding his tacit agreement.

"By the scruff of her skinny neck, figuratively, at least. And I invited her *not* to come back." Another glance at Nicole, who stood as if she, too, were carved of stone, stripped the stridence from her. "I'm sorry. Even a good customer isn't worth the trouble she causes."

Nicole dared not trust her voice, and answered with only the smallest inclination of her head. But for the first time since Matthew had begun his inquisition, she relented as Jeb drew her back against him, letting his arms offer respite from the hatefulness and spite of an avaricious woman.

Leaning into his embrace, reinforcing her stamina with his, she savored the warmth that reached into her. Mrs. Atherton's appalling insinuations didn't matter. They never should have. What she felt for Jeb, and the time they'd shared on Eden, would be shameful and ugly only if she let herself feel shameful and ugly.

He'd made no promises, nor had she. Yet neither regretted an enchanted sojourn in the sun-scattered shade of a cabana on a perfect day in paradise.

It was enough, and she was content.

Ashley would be found, she'd known he would be from the moment Matthew Sky smiled at her and promised. Then she would make him understand, and all would be well. She would make it so.

"That's it then? All he said, exactly as he said it?" Annabelle finished recounting her story, and Matthew was speaking, but Nicole had heard little of it. But there was something in Matthew's voice. Something that made her belief stronger.

"I had forgotten, until this minute." Annabelle scowled, she couldn't believe her outrage had blocked this one small but important incident in the havoc Mrs. Atherton brought down on them. "Ashley said, 'friend, best friend,' then something about new best friends. That's when he smashed his paintings."

Matthew slid back his chair and stood. He was tall for an Apache, taller than Jeb, and far, far, taller than Annabelle as he offered his hand. "Thank you." Her small white fingers were lost in his copper-skinned grasp. "Memory can be a capricious thing, particularly under stress. I know this was difficult for you, but you've been a lot of help. And whether you believe it or not, this saved us time."

"Just like that, out of the blue, you know where Ashley is?" Her arched eyebrows mirrored the shape of her heart-shaped forehead.

"Just like that, but not out of the blue." Matthew allowed himself one small grin, and his hard face was transformed into one of astonishing beauty. Not one inch of it anything but ruggedly masculine and perfect.

It was a measure of her guilt and worry that Annabelle didn't notice. Any other day, she would have groveled, not completely tongue in cheek, at his feet. "How do you know? What did I say?"

"I'll explain, I promise. But later. It will be dark in just a bit, and I'd like to go."

"I'll go with you," Nicole and Annabelle said in unison.

Jeb said nothing. Years in The Black Watch, and countless assignments with Matthew had taught him the uncanny tracker tracked alone.

"Better you wait here," Matthew explained. "He's hiding. He's been hurt, like a wild animal he's gone to ground to salve his wounds. If he sees either of you, he'll only try to run away again."

"You're right, I should have realized." Nicole kept her voice low, holding back the anguish that Ashley would feel so badly toward her he would hide from her. "Where will you look?"

Matthew flashed a breathtaking smile as he was leaving. "The zoo, of course."

"Of course," Nicole echoed, and it all made perfect sense.

Ashley was dirty and unkempt. A bewildered mix of belligerence and contrition. He'd skinned a knee and lost what he called his picture bag with the art supplies Nicole had given him. That he trusted Matthew and no one else was made painfully clear by the way he clung to the darker man's hand.

"Ashley." At the sound of Nicole's voice, he cringed behind Matthew, unable to understand that his bulk couldn't be hidden by a more slender frame. "I've missed you. Are you all right?"

At the much awaited peal of the bell at the door, Nicole had practically leapt from her desk. She'd spent the hours of waiting trying to work, to occupy her thoughts, to hurry the time. Now pages of columns of figures that eluded her scattered over its surface as she waited and hoped for his reply.

Biting her lip to hold back tears, Annabelle watched from the window where she'd kept her vigil.

From his seat a little distance away, Jeb's sole reaction was a long, appraising look at the childish resentment in Ashley's face, and the remorse in Nicole's. The only sound was the rustle of the journal he crumpled in his hand.

"Ashley, you promised," Matthew scolded in the tone a parent reserved for a much loved child. "Remember?"

Ashley jerked his head side to side. Lower lip quivering, he hunched lower trying to avoid Nicole's eyes.

"I'm sorry you're angry with me. I'd like to explain that my friendship with Jeb isn't like Mrs. Atherton said. It isn't—"

"Bad." Ashley pointed an accusing finger. "Do bad things."

Color drained from Nicole's face, her hands trembled, until she folded them before her. She should have been warned by Annabelle's reluctance to repeat the vitriolic tirade, but she wasn't prepared for this. "No, Ashley, Mrs. Atherton is wrong. You're wrong."

Her cry fell on deaf ears. Ashley stared stonily above her head. She'd seen him fall into this self-induced trance before when he refused to deal with something.

"All right, you don't have to talk to me if you don't want to." She'd been so sure she could make him understand. Now Nicole wondered if she could reach Ashley at all, ever again.

"Maybe he doesn't have to talk," Matthew said as he turned, taking the huge man by his massive shoulders, shaking him, commanding his attention. "But he has to listen, because he promised. And Ashley never breaks a promise."

Darting eyes found Jeb, a pout drew down a dirty lip.

"Jeb's here," Matthew said firmly. "I told you he would be. I told you why. He's a friend, and friends try to make you feel better when you feel sad. Nicole and Annabelle were feeling sad because you listened to a woman who wasn't your friend or theirs, and ran away."

"Matthew," Nicole interjected quietly. "He can't understand, it's too abstract."

"He understands and he'll understand even more." Taking a massive hand, Matthew led his charge toward the lounge. "I'm going to help you clean up, and bandage your scratches, Ashley. While I do, Nicole will collect some more paints for you, and maybe even a new bag for them. Then when we're all done, you're going to listen like you promised, and she'll explain everything.

"Just remember that she's your friend, she has been for a long time, and she always will be. But only you can decide if you want to be *her* friend."

The door to the lounge had hardly closed behind them when Annabelle erupted in a quiet, deadly rage. A low stream of epithets and threats, some old, some just invented, poured from her. The mildest of which was stitching Mrs. Old Biddy's mouth shut and making her spend the remainder of her life eating and drinking through a straw. The most violent, and to Annabelle the most satisfying, involved stripping her naked, hanging her upside down in the old slave market and leaving her for the world to see just how ugly she was, inside and out.

"I'll bet her favorite pastime when she was a little girl was pulling the wings off butterflies." Annabelle delivered one last salvo. "She must have been a horror in the barnyard."

Nicole had said nothing. Now, as she fumbled for her chair and sank down in it, she responded absently. "I doubt Mrs. Atherton has ever seen a barnyard."

"More's the pity," Annabelle grumbled. "She certainly belongs in one. And I know just the place. The pigpen."

Jeb barely listened as he struggled with the dilemma of needing to go to Nicole, to comfort her, and knowing it would only make things worse. He'd been as angry at the rumormonger as Annabelle. But was he any better?

He hadn't lied, but he hadn't been honest. Not with Nicole. Not with himself. Now he'd brought even more disorder and misery to her life than he ever intended.

And still there would be more the day Tony Callison came to her. The day she discovered the man she had given herself to—heart, soul, mind and body, without reservation—was an opportunist. A dishonest man, a greedy man.

Nicole sat in the darkness, in a darker world. Even the moon and stars had deserted her. The surf lapping at the shore beyond her house failed to soothe her.

The last hour in the gallery had been a horror. Ashley wouldn't listen. The entire time she'd spent trying to reach him, he'd sat staring into the distance. As immutable as stone, as unforgiving as the self-righteous.

Matthew, who had called heavily on the mystical rapport he shared with children and animals to find Ashley and bond with him, could not reason with him then.

Arguing brought little response. Pleading even less. Ashley was a child in the throes of a punishing sulk. Too young in mind to listen to reason, too mature in body to discipline. In the end she'd admitted defeat and, in language she prayed he'd understand, she'd given him his choices and explained their consequences. He could accept her friends and be her friend, or not. She'd been a part of his life for years, and he of hers. She would miss him if he continued as he was. Her one wish was that in denying her, he wouldn't deny his talent. The rest she'd left to him, the final choice was his.

Against her every hope, Ashley left the gallery without speaking. Even worse, he left the new bag of paints and supplies.

Jeb had withdrawn as quickly. A sympathetic look, a compassionate touch, and he was gone, with Matthew a step behind.

Many sleepless hours later, she moped on the steps of her deck in a night as somber as her mood. A surrogate mother who had lost her jealous child.

A lonely woman without her lover.

"So much for that." Rising from the steps, with her hands shoved deeply into the pockets of her jeans, she wandered the sand. She had no destination in mind, but her footsteps turned toward the ruin.

His report to Simon complete, Jeb sat with his head down, his hands lying limply on his knees. He'd delayed longer than he should to confirm that Nicole knew nothing of her brother, nor had she had any contact with him in years. That she'd offered the information without prompting made it more credible. The truthful sort of thing that could have come up in any conversation, anytime, anywhere.

The journey to Eden wasn't necessary, it needn't have happened. But it had. He was left to deal with it, and he had no idea how.

A radio beeped. Matthew was speaking before he lifted it from the table. ". . . walking toward the ruin. Shouldn't be alone. Should I call Mitch?"

"No," Jeb responded. "He should stay with the *Gambler,* we can't be sure when we might need it. Simon's convinced our quarry is moving again. The Merino family has stepped up the search for him, he's down to his last option. The only one he ever had. Watch the house, Matthew. I'll see to the lady."

Under the cover of darkness he started down the beach. He knew he needn't be concerned about Matthew. By rotating between two stations, every angle of Nicole's house was visible. No one could approach without alerting the canny Apache. Mitch would be as responsible with the *Gambler.* That left Jeb and his responsibility.

Nicole.

He saw her ahead, a shadowy form in the nearly unrelieved black of the night. Keeping a steady pace that wouldn't alarm her, he reached the base of the ruin seconds after she scaled the slanting stones.

"Jogging this late, Jeb?" Her voice floated down to him, flat, without inflection.

"I came to see about you." The truth, as far as it went.

"What about me?"

"Have you heard from Ashley?"

"No."

"Do you expect to?"

"No."

"Can you say anything but no?"

"Such as?"

"Such as come join me."

"All right," she said with the same apathy. "If that's what you want to hear, come join me."

"Thought you'd never ask."

When he climbed the ruin with an enviable ease, he sat beside her. Her legs were drawn up, her arms wrapped around them, her chin rested on her knees. She stared out to sea, at a flashing buoy.

"Tough day." He touched her cheek, regretting the livid scratch.

"I've had better."

Unable to stop himself, he stroked her hair. His hand wandered to her shoulders, finding the taut muscles. His fingers were skillful, soothing. "I'm sorry. For everything."

"Don't. Don't be kind and don't touch me." Despite her command, she didn't move from him.

"Why not, sweetheart?" A fingertip trailed down her spine.

She drew an unsteady breath. "Because I don't want to fight you, or myself."

He gathered her hair in his palm, turning her gaze to his. "Then why fight at all?"

"Because..."

His lips brushed over hers, warm, caressing. "Because?"

"Because..."

He kissed her again, his tongue teasing the sweet inner softness of her mouth and lifting away. "You were saying?"

"Was I?" He'd walked away from her a second time, but it didn't matter. He was here now, and he cared, she heard it in his voice, felt it in his touch. Her arms crept about his eck, her fingers burrowed in his hair as she brought him back to her. "I can't seem to remember."

"Neither can I," he murmured into her kiss as he drew her down with him to the marble of Folly's Castle.

He hadn't planned this, not consciously, but he couldn't say he hadn't wanted it. On another, primal level, he'd known from the moment he stepped on the shore that he would make love to her.

Like a greedy man stealing one last taste of heaven, while fires of hell licked at his soul, he would make love to her.

If she would have him.

Her yielding body curling into his was his answer.

And the clock in his head ticked down to disaster.

Nine

"**A**nything?"

Nicole looked up from a small bronze, her eyes focusing on Annabelle as she rushed through the door. Her mind was a beat behind, assimilating the abbreviated question. "I'm sorry." She frowned at the curio case with other similar bronzes arranged on its shelves. "What did you say?"

"I was asking about Ashley," Annabelle answered. She hadn't bothered with good morning, or how are you, because it wasn't a good morning, and how Nicole was showed in the haggard lines on her face. "You haven't heard from him, or had any news."

"Nothing," Nicole answered in a tight voice, though the latter was an observation, not a question. "Three days, and nothing. This time even Matthew found no trace."

"For a while late yesterday, Harry thought he might have seen him down by the Ashley river bridge. He never got close enough to see for sure, but Ashley wouldn't stray that far away from his familiar grounds. At least, not as a rule." Nicole's instant disappointment dragged Annabelle's spirit another notch lower. "Anyway, turned out there were two of them. From a distance, looked like two old guys basking in the sun.''

"He was hiding before, gone to ground. I'm afraid he is again, even from Matthew. But for so long?''

Annabelle made a clucking sound and heaved her shoulders. "Who knows what the poor, confused man could be thinking.''

"More than that, Annabelle, how is he living? The few dollars he made shining shoes bought the little he needed, now he hasn't been around to earn even that much. I talked with the grocer who helps him with his money and supplies, and even the barber who shaves him and cuts his hair. Neither has seen Ashley.''

"There's something you need to consider.''

"I know, but not yet.'' Nicole leaned her head briefly in her hand. A customer who browsed just out of earshot looked up, clearly aware of her distress though she didn't understand it, then good manners got the better of curiosity and she turned away again.

"Waiting won't make it any easier.'' Softly, as a mother would, she said what must be said. "We may never see Ashley again. He's never in his life been able to keep an idea in his head long enough to bear a grudge, but this time might be different.''

"I'd hoped not.'' Nicole closed the glass doors of the cabinet with a sharp thud.

"We all hoped it was a tempest in a teapot. Something he would get over like a disappointed schoolboy's crush.''

"But he hasn't. I hoped painting would lure him back and I tried to leave that door open, at least. Jeb has stayed away, thinking it would help.''

"So that's why he's been conspicuously absent.''

In Charleston and at the gallery, maybe, but not on the island. Every time she looked up, or took a step, Jeb was there. If not Jeb, then one of his crew. Mitch and Matthew had never been as visible as they were now.

"We both thought it best.'' Nicole moved away from Annabelle's perceptive gaze. She'd run an emotional gamut for three days, and her astute assistant was certain to see.

"Just like it was best he walked out of here when you needed someone. No," Annabelle amended, "when you needed him." She would be some time forgetting he'd walked away from Nicole. She'd made no bones about it over the days since.

"Jeb felt that by being here, he was responsible for how badly it turned out."

A group of customers poured into the gallery. Nicole prayed they would prove a distraction, ending the conversation. But beyond responding to her greeting, they continued to laugh and talk among themselves. Annabelle's unwelcome attention remained on her.

"You *think*," Annabelle said, moving closer, her hands on her hips, dark eyes flashing. "You don't know."

"But I do know, Annabelle."

"Has he told you?"

"Not exactly."

"Then how?"

"I know Jeb. That's enough."

"Do you?" Through narrowed eyes she watched Nicole, as if by shutting out the rest of their surroundings she would discover some enlightening truth. But, oddly, she felt the truth hadn't been written, yet. "I wonder if you do. I wonder if anyone knows Jeb Tanner." Then thoughtfully, "I wonder if Jeb Tanner knows Jeb Tanner."

A customer chose that time to ask for information about some small bauble, something to take home to his wife. Nicole gratefully addressed his question, and a pattern was set. It was the last day of a convention, husbands and lovers who'd spent their days on golf courses, the tennis courts, deep sea fishing and even occasionally the convention, rushed in to buy the definitive gift that would prove how hard they'd worked, and how much the loved one had been missed.

Nicole didn't question the hypocrisy, or quarrel with it, she was simply thankful to be too occupied to think on Annabelle's last observation. By the end of the day, she was exhausted. For one brief moment she considered staying over in the Charleston, then realized that would make her too easily accessible to Annabelle. She loved the woman dearly, but tonight she wasn't ready for any more of her incisive analysis. It was a distinct possibility that the same incisiveness could be brought to the island. Annabelle was certainly familiar with it, and all its news. But the island had a deterrent Charleston didn't.

"...Jeb?"

Nicole whirled from her last chore of the day to stare at Annabelle. Her first thought was that Annabelle had finished a thought she'd spoken aloud; her second, that this clever woman who seemed attuned to her had added mind reading to her skills. Then she realized it was only a question.

"Hey!" Annabelle backed away from Nicole's hard, intense look. "I was only asking. You act as if I committed a sin."

"I'm sorry, I was thinking of something else, I didn't really hear you."

"There's a lot you don't hear lately. Or see."

"What does that mean?"

"Be switched if I know. Just a passing thought. But you will be seeing him tonight, right?"

"Jeb."

"Who else?"

"He usually drops by sometime during the evening."

"For what reason?"

"Does he have to have a reason?"

"Most people do."

"I'll be sure to ask him," Nicole said dryly.

"You do that. The answer might surprise both of you."

Nicole refused to ask what the cryptic remark meant. "You don't like him very much now, do you?"

"Are you kidding?" Eyebrows rose theatrically. "As far as I'm concerned, its a toss up to decide which of the three of them is the hottest number to come to town in a long, long while."

"You didn't answer my question, Annabelle."

"Let's just say the jury's out on that question, and leave it at that, shall we?" To make sure Nicole didn't press her for an answer she couldn't give, Annabelle gathered up her keys. "If that's all for the day, I'd like to get on home. Harry's making a special dinner."

Nicole was quick to grasp this straw that offered escape. Their conversation was going nowhere. "Let's both go home," she suggested. "And forget this day."

Dressed in slacks, a long flowing shirt and barefoot, Nicole tarried in her kitchen, spending more time putting away food she'd prepared, than she had eating. In Annabelle's words, she'd skinnied down some in the past week or so, but she hadn't bothered with stepping on the scales after her shower. She'd worry about her weight when there was nothing else to worry about.

A tread on the stairs leading from the beach signaled what she'd been waiting for. She was at the door, sliding it open, by the time he stepped on the deck.

She thought he would kiss her as he had the other evenings he'd finished his nightly stroll with dropping by her house. Instead, grim-faced and without a word, he slipped his arms around her, and tugged her to him. His fingers ruffled through her hair, drawing her cheek to his chest. His embrace was tight, hard, the slow, easy beat of an athlete's heart played a steady rhythm in her ear.

He held her so tightly, so silently, alarm crept through her immediate pleasure. "Jeb?"

She would have struggled to lift her head, but his lips were there at her crown, brushing light kisses over dark tresses. "Shh," he ordered, his warm breath rushing over her. "Just for now don't think, don't worry, just let me hold you."

She didn't understand, she hadn't for some time, but nothing in the world would have kept her from answering the strange, fierce hunger she heard in his voice. Slipping her arms around him, she nestled closer, filling her lungs with the crisp, clean scent of him. Alarm quieted, lulled by the sure, vital strength of the heart beneath her cheek, the arms that held her. Her mind drifted, blocking out thought and worry. Her body softened, responded.

As if he'd been waiting for this moment, needed it, he muttered softly and held her closer in a dance without steps, with only the sound of the sea for their music. There was feverish desperation in his touch as if he would never let her go. Yet, after a minute, he murmured something unintelligible and relaxed his embrace.

Nicole stepped back, hoping she wouldn't see the haunted look that had become disturbingly familiar. Yet knowing she would.

"You look tired, sweetheart." Jeb stroked circles like bruises under her eye, wishing this ordeal were over. That Tony Callison would come, not within the few days projected, but now. Then he could get out of her life, and she could restore what order she could.

All the gentleness left him as he lifted his gaze from her face, letting it sweep the room as if he were searching for something that should be there. Something abominable.

His eyes were cold, icily perceptive.

Gray ice.

Nicole shivered, every vestige of warmth fled from her. Stunned by the meteoric transformation, she stepped back again. As she looked away, a brutally honest part of her admitted the change in him wasn't so stunning after all. It had begun with the restless watchfulness. Perhaps it had always been there, but she hadn't been so keenly aware of it until the super-cautious approach to Eden.

Restless. The day she'd warned Annabelle he was restless and would sail away one day, loomed like a ghostly specter. A reasonable warning, for Annabelle, for herself. But her heart hadn't listened.

Jeb's gaze returned to her. He saw her pallor, the tremble of her lips. The stark hurt in glittering eyes that branded his soul with a look that matched the mood that had plagued him all day.

She knows. The thought struck him like a thunderbolt. Not what I am, he thought, but what I can never be.

"I'm sorry," he whispered. She knew, but didn't understand what she knew. But she would when this was done. "I shouldn't have come."

"Jeb..."

He didn't mean to touch her again. But he found himself taking the hand that reached out to him. A small hand, delicate, but not fragile. Like the woman. She would be all right in time.

Time. There would never be any for him. Only to say goodbye.

"Rest, sweetheart. This will be over soon."

"What?" Her hand convulsed in his. "No!"

"Shh," he soothed. Lifting her hand to his lips he kissed her fingers. As he released her he stepped back. Lover had become hunter, as he always should have been. The smile that curved his lips gently did not touch his eyes.

Forgive me.

Long after his footsteps were swallowed by the night, the words fluttered in her mind like moth wings. Hushed, surreal. Had he said them, or had she only imagined?

Dry-eyed, she stared into the darkness, as still as stone, as blind. Hours might have passed, or only minutes, when she roused. She didn't know or care.

Forgive me.

He'd made no promises, she'd wanted none.

For a while she'd been happier than she ever thought she could be. What did that leave to forgive? Nicole turned her back on the brooding darkness.

"There's nothing, Jeb. Nothing that needs forgiveness."

Matthew caught the first hint of movement at the edge of his vision. A clump of sea oats shuddered where there was no wind. Sand tumbled without reason from the top of a dune. If he were a man given to assumption, his first would have been a foraging animal. His second that Jeb had returned.

The Watch lived by fact, and died by assumption.

Swinging the night glasses toward the disturbance and holding his breath, he waited. Nothing. Still he waited. His hand itched for the radio.

"Not yet," he muttered. Sweat trickled in his eyes. He didn't blink or wipe it away. Another stem of oats shook, the heavy head shivering in still air. Sand slipped in a miniature avalanche, this time closer to the house. His eyes strained.

Nothing.

The Apache word for patience rolled softly off his tongue. Then, as if assimilated by refracted light, a figure appeared at the base of the first piling of Nicole's house. Matthew reached for the radio, as instinct and intuition sounded a silent warning.

A rare curse ripped from him.

His face was hard, his eyes angry slits, his lips a cruel slash when he finally spoke. "Jeb."

Jeb was lying in the dark, staring at the ceiling, damning the long hours of waiting. His name sliced through his thoughts, a disembodied whisper summoning him from hell. In one fluid move he was on his feet, listening.

"He's here." The radio hissed its alarm.

Every nerve and muscle was honed, ready, in a chaotic mix of relief and fear. "Where?"

"Close enough that he'll be inside in thirty seconds."

Jeb grabbed a shirt. "I'm on my way."

"Jeb! There's more." Matthew's urgent voiced crackled through the room. "Listen."

With a sinking feeling that turned to rage, Jeb listened.

Nicole stirred as something scratched at her mind, drawing her from her shallow sleep. She'd slept fitfully, dreaming of riddles with no answers, waking often. Yet never as completely as now. Never with the feeling of . . .

What?

She knew only that her heart was racing, her skin prickled with the feel of eyes watching from the dark.

A whisper of sound barely beyond her bed set a shock wave spiraling through her. Her heart lurched, a painful pressure stabbed her chest. Her mouth was dry, her throat too taut to scream. Sitting upright in a jerky motion, not out of boldness, but because she couldn't face the unknown lying down, she called a name in a labored voice, and prayed. "Jeb?"

A mirthless chuckle flowed out of a shadow darker than the rest, a hollow sound, plucking at her nerves like a guitar string tuned too tightly. "Not this time, Nicole. But I've brought someone else to see you."

It took a minute for recognition to penetrate the befuddling haze of fear. Gathering the covers to her breasts, she sat up, willing herself to see through murky shade. This was crazy! It couldn't be. "Tony?"

"Right, the second try." He moved soundlessly, his body seeming to materialize in a pool of light falling from the window. Nicole choked back a cry as she found herself looking at an older, masculine version of herself. As she stared, he laughed again. "What? Nothing to say to your long lost brother?"

She couldn't think, couldn't feel. There was only confusion. Striving to make sense of this, of his sudden appearance, and his obvious need for secrecy, she forced herself to be calm. Only her fingers twitched nervously against the covers. "What should I say?"

"You're a cool one now, aren't you? No bloodcurdling shrieks of fright, no happy tears. So, how about 'long time, no see'?" He lounged against the chair at the foot of her bed. "There was a time you would've run to me, wrapping yourself around my neck like a limpet."

"Limpet." The word battered at her, repelled her. "Is that what I was to you? All I was?"

"Eventually. Why else do you think I walked away from you, with your diploma clutched so proudly in your hand, all those years ago?"

Nicole felt sick, and she felt foolish carrying on a conversation from her bed. Throwing back the sheet, not caring that her shirt stopped short of her knees, she slipped into her robe. "Let's continue this conversation, if that's what it is, in the other room, shall we?"

This was her brother. She'd spent the greater part of her life worshiping him. Now she was speaking to him as if he were a stranger and denying the excoriating pain his words inflicted after a lifetime removed from him.

She was shaking and dazed as she walked past him and into the next room. She was afraid that if he touched her she would scream. Her brother! Dear God, she was afraid of her brother!

"Don't!" His command lashed out of the darkness as she fumbled for the light switch. "No lights, please. The moonlight's so much cozier for an old-fashioned family re-union, don't you think?''

Nicole sank to the sofa, her strength sapped by the harsh command, the scornful mockery. ''What do you want, Tony?'' She was shivering and horrified that all she felt for him was mistrust and dread. Wrapping her arms tightly about herself she forced an even tone into her voice. ''Why are you here, like this? Why now?''

''You don't know?'' He leaned against the doorjamb, watching her. ''He hasn't told you?''

''He?'' She felt dense, disconnected, as if she'd come into the middle of a very bad movie.

''Your new boyfriend, who else?''

''Jeb?''

''Ahh, a little honesty, at last.''

''What would Jeb tell me about you, Tony? He's never mentioned you more than once or twice. What would he know about you? You haven't seen each other in fifteen years, what could he say?''

''Now isn't that strange? Considering what close buddies we were and he never mentioned me, never asked about me. But you didn't notice, did you? Too starry-eyed? Why would he mention me?'' The soft unctuous voice dropped to a low snarl. ''Because he's a cop, sugar. Do you hear me, a cop!''

''That's insane.'' Her nails were sharp and piercing against the tender flesh of her arms. She moved her head violently side to side. To clear it, to deny, she didn't know. ''Jeb's retired. He made his fortune in stocks and bonds.''

''Sure, and he just happened to retire a continent away from his home, on the island my sister just happens to live on, as well.'' A grimace drew down his mouth. A bizarre, wooden expression, as if any feeling was a travesty. ''Makes a nice fairy tale, wouldn't you say?''

''You're guessing. You don't know for sure.''

''I don't have to know for sure. And I don't have to know who he's working for, what private or public sector, or even if he's legit at all. I know the breed when I see it.'' He caught her quick look of dismay. ''Hit a nerve, did I? You've wondered a little about him yourself. Like what's a man like him doing here, with a crew like his?''

Another conversation came back to haunt her. She could close her eyes and hear Annabelle expounding about Jeb Tanner, the man of mystery. Asking who really knew him. Nicole bit her lip. She hadn't known him. Not even a little.

"You've been used, sugar. Whoever he works for was smart enough to figure you were my last option. All old Jeb had to do was weasel into your good graces, and from the looks of things, your pants, then sit back and wait for me."

Nicole hugged herself tighter, and felt sicker. She wouldn't think of Jeb, what he had done or why. "What have *you* done, Tony? Why would the authorities, or whoever, want you?"

"A long story. If I'd needed you to know, I wouldn't have walked away from you in the first place."

"That long?" She raised startled eyes to his and found them lackluster in the half-light. "What you've done was that long ago?"

"For that long," he corrected, letting her understand it wasn't a one time thing. No childish prank, nor one single thoughtless act.

"If you knew he was here waiting for you, why did you come?"

"You haven't been listening, little sister. You're my last option. The last person I could turn to."

"That can't be true."

"But it is." He stepped from the door, moving closer.

"There's nothing I can do."

"You're wrong." Moonlight spilling through tall windows was like a pale, wintry sun. In its light she saw that he was older than his years, and seedy. Desperation radiated from him like a rank odor. And something more, something off kilter.

"You've just decided you need some time off." He spun a tale for her. "You're going to charter a boat with a crew to sail the Caribbean Islands. Makes sense, you like islands."

"Where would you be in the meantime? While plans are made?"

"Right here, where else?"

"What would I tell Jeb?"

"From what I've seen, you and your new lover quarreled."

"You've been watching me!" The thought of those odd eyes peering at her from hidden places made her cringe.

Beyond a feral grin, Tony ignored her outburst. "You tell him you don't want to see him anymore, that you're going away to heal your broken heart."

"If he won't accept that?"

A gun appeared in Tony's hand. A monstrous weapon. A magnum, chrome and black and lethal as a cannon. "Then we'll settle it with this."

Panic started deep in her chest and exploded. "You can't!"

"Wanna bet?" He looked at her with an unchanging gaze, pointed a finger at her head and pulled an imaginary trigger. At her smothered gasp, his mouth moved in a caricature of a laugh, the sound sending snakes slithering down her spine. "I won't hurt you, Nicole, but you will help me. Shall I show you why?"

Only a simpleton wouldn't have known then what her brother's crimes were, and why it was so crucial he escape. Horror sizzled through panic. Terror for Jeb turned it deadly calm. In the throes of cartwheeling sensation she managed to say almost conversationally, "I won't help you, Tony. I want you to leave, disappear from my life as completely as you did before. Forget you ever had a sister. And I'll try my damnedest to forget you."

Tony clucked his tongue, and chucked her under the chin. He grinned when she didn't recoil. "You found some guts over the years, have you? Or is all this bravado for your lover's sake?"

She met his scorn levelly. "It isn't bravado for anyone."

"You think he loves you? Wise up. He came here to betray you, and whatever he's done, however sweet he's been—" sarcasm curled his mouth into a nasty leer "—it was only to get to me. Then he'll walk, as far and fast as he can. As he must have countless times before, from countless women as gullible."

Nicole didn't respond. Jeb had already walked. To the *Gambler* and out to sea with his crew, she prayed.

"Gonna be stubborn?" Tony laughed again. He laughed too much, an off note that wasn't quite right. And when she let her gaze settle on him, his head jerked and he was first to look away. "I think it's time to play my ace in the hole. See how stubborn you are then."

He stepped to the deck and disappeared into the darkest corner. A thud, the crack of an open-handed slap was followed by a low, mournful wail that brought new fear leaping into Nicole's heart. She was on her feet, afraid to look, but afraid to look away when Tony shoved a cowering, sobbing giant into the room.

"Ashley!" His name was all she had time to say as he sprawled at her feet. A murderous look thrown over her shoulder cut short an unnatural bark of laughter as she knelt by the rigid man.

A handkerchief threaded through his lips, dragging his chin back at an awkward angle. His hands were bound, the flesh turning a ghastly color from too little circulation for too long. She touched his cheeks, wiping tears from them. She spoke softly, comfortingly, but Ashley didn't see her or hear her. He didn't feel the soiled gag loosen and slide away. Response was beyond him for he'd slipped into the self-induced trance that was his only protection from horrors he didn't understand.

Nicole stood; without a glance at Tony, with her back straight and her chin at a fighting angle she stalked to the kitchen.

"Where do you think you're going?"

She turned, her eyes were as gray and cold as Jeb's had been. "I don't think, I know where I'm going. First I'm going to turn on a lamp, then I'm going to the kitchen for a knife to cut Ashley free."

Tony lifted the gun, the muzzle centered on her.

"You want to shoot me? Then do it. But who will you turn to if you do? Jeb's out there somewhere. So is Mitch Ryan, a Cajun who can laugh in one breath and cut your heart out the next. And with them is a master tracker, an Apache called Matthew Winter Sky. Once he has your scent, he'll find you no matter where you go, or how far. When he does, if you've hurt Ashley, you'll regret it more than you've regretted anything in your life.

"Without me you don't stand a chance, Tony. So make up your mind. Shoot or turn the gun away." She knew she should be frightened out of her skull, but she was too furious to care. "While you're making up your mind, I'm going to cut Ashley free before he loses his hands."

She saw a finger squeeze against the trigger.

"There's only me, Tony," she said softly. "Or you wouldn't be here. Only me, or you wouldn't risk facing Jeb." Her voice sank to a singsong rhythm, "Only me, only me." She could feel the bullet in her chest, feel his need to put it there.

This was her brother!

She caught back a moan of despair and tried to rekindle a lost kinship. "There's me, Tony. Only your sister."

"Shut up!" The gun wavered and steadied. No life shone from blank eyes, but there was sweat on his forehead. His shrug was stiff, unnatural. "Turn on the lamp, get the knife. Cut your pet fool free. But know this, and believe me, if he makes one suspicious move, he's fish bait."

Nicole met him stare for stare, then, turning on her heel, she walked when she wanted to run. She'd gained an edge, a small one she must keep at all costs. One overt sign of the terror that lay twisted in her ready to spin out of control and she would lose everything. Ashley's life, her own. Jeb's.

The knife was slippery in her hand as she knelt again by Ashley. He hadn't moved, he didn't blink in the bright light of the lamp. For once Nicole was grateful for the self-induced trance she'd once thought maddening. Sawing at the rope, trying not to cut skin that had already torn in his struggle against captivity, a part of her knew the horror Ashley felt. He hated to be caged or closed in. Being tied and gagged would be as bad.

Ashley would have begged and cried, and struggled however long it took. The varying age of the bruises on his face and hands spoke of days. She wondered if the monster who held a gun at her back had laughed his monster's laugh.

More hate and revulsion than she knew she could feel burned through her. A conflagration that purged her fear, leaving only cold eyed, bitter rage.

She dropped the knife, the bonds were cut. Ashley lay as he was. Only tears spilling on his cheeks told her that the excruciating pain of blood rushing through starved vessels penetrated his fog.

"Lie still, Ashley," she whispered. "Dear heaven, please lie still."

"Shut up."

"You said you didn't want him to move. That's what I'm telling him." She brushed the shaggy, dirty hair from Ashley's face. "It doesn't matter how big his body is, or how old he is, he's a child."

"Cuts no ice with me. Big, small, old, young, I've killed children before."

Nicole jerked around, staring up at him. Hate and rage rose a notch.

He saw it. Laughed. And when she shivered at the sound, he laughed again. "It occurs to me it would simplify matters if we had another reunion. You know, old surfing buddies, Sons of Apollo."

"No!" She would have risen, flown at his face, his eyes, with her nails if Ashley hadn't chosen that moment to move, to try to rise. With a strength born of desperation she forced the huge man back, soothing him with a touch and a soft word as he subsided.

"My, my, my, you do have the magic touch. Old Jeb must've purred. Let's get him over here, I'd like to ask him what it was like. Call him."

She settled back on her heels, one hand touching Ashley. Eyes so similar collided, one pair dead, cold, the other just as cold, but alive and unyielding. "No!"

"That's your favorite word, isn't it? Except with Mr. Golden Boy. You had a crush on him way back, it's a little more now, huh?" He prodded her with the gun. She looked away rigidly. He turned her back with the barrel at her cheek. "Call him."

"Don't be a fool, you don't need Jeb here. I'm all you need." The same old verse, but this time he didn't listen.

With the metallic sight he traced a cruel line along the path of the scratch, opening the newly healed flesh. Blood trickled on her robe. "Call him."

She jerked away from the cold, oily feel of the gun. Her look lashed out with all that seethed inside her. "No."

A blow spun her around. If it had been with the gun, her face would have split open, his open hand only bruised. "Call."

"There's no need to call. I'm here." Jeb stepped through the door left open when Tony dragged Ashley from the deck. His hands were empty, raised. "If you touch her again, I'll kill you with my bare hands."

A promise, not a threat, made in a flat voice. A matter of fact, as inevitable as the rising sun. Only a fool wouldn't have believed.

Blood dripped from Nicole's cheek, falling over Ashley's grubby shirt. In the shaded light of the lamp it glittered like black oil. Every drop hurting Jeb.

Stay down, Nicky.

He didn't look at her as he eased his arms down. He couldn't take the risk. "You wanted me here, Tony, now I am. So?"

The laugh. Something not quite human from a husk that had been a human being. The sound filled Jeb with loathing, and with dread. His last, slim hope to end this without disaster or tragedy fled. The tragedy was already here. It stood before him in the guise of a man who had been his friend.

Tony sobered, the gun pointed steadily at Jeb. "Since this is my little sister, I wanted a look at the man who'd been—"

"Don't say it." Jeb's deadly command cut him off before the vulgarity spilled out.

"Ahh, you want flowery phrases for it do you? To make it all nice and proper. Maybe you should ask Nicole's fool here just how nice and proper both of you are."

Tony was goading him, wanting him to make a move. It made about as much sense as floating a cork in a hurricane. Jeb looked into the familiar face, reading what experience had taught him was there. The confidence, the arrogance. In Tony's convoluted thoughts, he'd gotten to Nicole clean. No one had seen him. Jeb's coming was coincidence, and he'd come alone. Just dropping by at the late hour, hoping to catch her in bed so he might join her.

The lust a brother imagined, turned to blood lust. So he goaded Jeb to make a fatal move.

Tony was offtrack, irrational, spoiling his chances of escape to feed an unholy craving. And that much more unpredictable.

They weren't likely to leave this room without bloodshed. Blood Tony craved. But Jeb had to try. "You want to leave the country? I'll take you, if you leave Nicole and Ashley."

"Do I look like a fool? I might take you up on the boat ride, but if I do, my leverage goes with me." Without taking his eyes from Jeb, he leaned down enough to grab a handful of Nicole's hair. With a vicious twist he dragged her to her feet.

The scream she bit off was for Jeb as he lunged forward, a small weapon, drawn from the back of his belt, in his hand. It wasn't her aborted scream that stopped him, but Tony, for now the muzzle of his gun was pressed with bruising force to her throat.

Jeb backed away, hands up and open, the pistol hooked over his thumb. "Put it away, Tony. You're hurting her."

"No, you put it away." With his head, Tony motioned Jeb to toss the gun. "You can't shoot your lover's brother, anyway. Wouldn't make for family harmony. But then, there wouldn't be a family. If you take me down, in that split-second hesitation you worry about her..." The muzzle stabbed deeper into her throat. "Bang!"

Jeb hesitated, looking into Nicole's eyes drawn to slits by the pressure of Tony's grasp.

Be still, Nicky. Don't fight him.

"Do it!" Tony screamed and dragged her back a step, jerking her harder when she tripped over Ashley.

"You win." Slowly, Jeb bent to lay the gun at his feet.

"Never thought I wouldn't. Now, kick it away." The gun slid away. Tony laughed. "Get down on your knees."

Nicole knew what was coming. She knew what Tony meant to do. "No, please."

"Shh, Nicky. Everything's all right," Jeb assured as he dropped to the floor.

The gun swung toward him, the hammer was back.

Jeb saw Nicole tense.

Be still, love. Please be still.

"Say goodbye, sugar." He jerked her hair brutally, twisting her neck at an impossible angle. Blood from the opened scratch flew in spattering dots over the floor and Jeb. And Ashley. The groan she couldn't stifle ripped from her throat. Tony shook her again, and more blood fell.

Jeb saw him move. Muscles bunched, fingers like saplings clutched the knife, and the big body rose from the floor noiselessly, a three-hundred-pound zephyr. There was nothing Jeb could do as Ashley plowed into Tony, but go with him. Launching himself from the floor, he hooked an arm around Nicole's waist. In the deafening roar of gunshots he rolled with her across the floor as a dreadful drama played itself out in brutal vignettes.

A bullet shattered glass.

Jeb shielded Nicole with his body.

Shots.

A scream.

Mitch shouted, he was answered by Matthew.

Ashley fell heavily, brought down too late by Matthew's low tackle.

The blood of a man-child mingled with Jeb's.

A shot.

Tony laughed, then he cried.

Silence.

Footsteps crushed broken glass into the floor. In the acrid smoke, a figure knelt by Tony Callison. He pushed a sun-face medallion aside to search for a pulse at his throat. After a minute his hand lifted to his knee, but he did not rise.

"You thought Jeb couldn't do this, child killer?" Mitch Ryan's whisper barely rippled the silence. "I just beat him to it."

Ten

Red light strafed the night, painting leaf and limb and face the color of blood. The tinny voice of a radio babbled from the open door of an ambulance as white-coated figures raced a stretcher down a walk.

A life was slipping away.

Kiawah's gray-shirted security held back the scattering of onlookers as Nicole hurried to the street. At the ambulance door she paused, only a second, but long enough to see the solitary figure, the bloodred shadow that watched from the landing.

"Ma'am." A chivalrous hand took her arm. A face too young for the skills the mind and hand possessed looked solemnly down at her. "We're ready."

Nicole turned away from the watchful figure, not sure what she felt, or what she believed. A haze of grief and shock clouded her thoughts as she climbed obediently into the back of the vehicle. Huddling on a jump seat she stared down at her hands as the young man leapt in beside her.

She looked up as he cried, "Go!"

The last face she saw, as the light changed and the ambulance door slammed, was Jeb's.

Sirens moaned. Growled. Built to a banshee howl.
The race against time had begun.

An unearthly hush lay over the shore. The darkness was
lifting, but Jeb didn't notice. He'd stood for more than an
hour at the edge of the sea, shoulders slumped, hands deep
in his pockets, staring down at the water lapping at his feet.
A freshening breeze warned of a storm. Spray flew in a fine
mist, plastering his shirt to his chest. Stains ran pink, then
red, but he didn't care.

He wondered if he would ever care again.

"Jeb." As Matthew would with a friend, he warned before he touched. A dark, coppery hand rested on a damp
shoulder, gently but urgently. "It's time to go."

"To the hospital."

"Dr. Gordon will be waiting."

"To treat a flesh wound." Even a stabbing laceration
didn't hurt as badly as the look Nicole had given him when
she realized how seriously Ashley was injured.

"More than that, and better attended to now than later."

"How is Ashley?"

"He's in surgery. It looks bad, but he's a strong kid."
Kid. He was a man of fifty years, at least, but Matthew saw
only the heart and mind of a child.

"Nicole?"

"Bruised and battered. Grieving for the man her brother
was, but not the man who died on Kiawah. Her throat will
be sore for some time, her cheek will heal and the scar will
fade. Eventually, along with scars of a different sort. Physically, other than that, she's fine. Thanks to you."

"Sure," Jeb snarled. "She's lucky to have me in her life."

"I think so," Matthew answered mildly.

"Ask her. See if she agrees."

"Why don't you ask her, Jeb? The answer might surprise you."

"I don't think either of us believes that." And brave,
tough Jeb Tanner hadn't the guts to risk her answer.

Matthew didn't argue. He saw it was a waste of breath.
"Mitch will be finished with the coroner. He'll meet us at
the hospital."

"What arrangements will be made for Tony?"

"What happens after the official investigation will be up to Nicole."

"Yeah, I suppose it will. Whatever he was when he died, once upon a time, he was her brother." Jeb shoved his hands deeper in his pockets. "And my friend."

"No," Matthew refuted quietly. "The part of him who was her brother and your friend died a long time ago."

"What remained became a killer." Jeb faltered, his voice roughened. "He would have killed Nicole."

"When he didn't need her anymore."

Jeb nodded. Perhaps neither The Black Watch nor he could be absolved for hurting Nicole, but she never wore the sun-face medallion. She was alive, and one day she would be happy again. He had that to take with him.

"Ready?" Matthew's hand moved from his shoulder.

Jeb looked up at the sky. It would be dawn soon. "Yeah," he said as he turned his back to the sea. "I'm ready."

The hospital was white. The walls were white, the floors, the ceiling, the linens. The stretcher where Jeb lay while a surgeon stitched his forearm had been white.

"That should do it. You lost a lot of blood, would've lost more if Ryan hadn't applied the pressure bandage. But you're a lucky man, Mr. Tanner. Without that bracelet deflecting the blade, this would have severed a couple of tendons, and cost you the use of your fingers. I don't know what sort of work you do, but not many of us can afford the virtual loss of a hand. So there's fortune in your misfortune." Dr. Gordon, a middle-aged physician who'd seen more misfortune than he ever wanted to, took a prescription pad from his pocket, scratched something on it, scribbled his name at the bottom and ripped it from the pad.

"Knife wounds can be tricky, have this filled at the hospital pharmacy." He handed the folded paper to Jeb. "Take it easy for a while, until the blood you lost is regenerated, and take this religiously. Even good fortune sometimes needs help."

"Right." Jeb sat up, sliding into what was left of his shirt. He hadn't thought to change, now it was too late. He was a walking reminder of the everything Nicole needed to forget. But no help for it now. "Thanks, doc."

Dr. Gordon peered at him over his glasses. "You won't mind if I don't say 'any time'?"

Jeb laughed. He hadn't thought he could so soon. "I won't mind."

Saying he'd walked in, and he would walk out, Jeb refused the offer of a wheelchair and went in search of Nicole. He found her huddled in the corner of a waiting room. Mitch and Matthew were there. A small silent circle, together, but apart. When he appeared at the door, torn and bloodstained, a collective gasp rose from others who waited in their own anxious misery.

Only Nicole didn't look up. Only she didn't react.

Matthew's dark gaze found his, flicked over the bulky bandage at his arm and moved back to Nicole. A touch, a soft word, and he rose, with Mitch following.

Her lips moved in response to their kindness, but Jeb couldn't hear. As Matthew and Mitch passed him, he didn't look away from her bowed head, and only nodded at their parting wish of luck. His luck had run out. One look at her anguish was proof of it.

One by one, others found some urgent need to be somewhere. A bite to eat, a cup of coffee, a cigarette, the need to stretch cramped legs. One by one they drifted away, until there was only the sad, beautiful woman and the wounded, gray-eyed warrior.

"Nicky." He knelt at her feet, lifting her face with a touch at her chin. Her eyes were dark, as dark as a secret forest, heartache burned in them with a hot, green fire.

"I did this. He trusted me and…" Her voice drifted away, her sins too numerous and too terrible to recount.

"You're wrong."

"Don't." She held up a hand warding off his denial and stared blankly at the flickering screen of a television. "Let it be."

But he couldn't. "If you must condemn someone, why not everyone?" Then one after another he ticked off a multitude of transgressions. Real and imaginary, some intended, others sheer happenstance. "Why not Tony for firing the gun? Mitch for not risking a chancy shot and failing to taken Tony down quicker? Matthew for not finding Ashley's trail? Harry for not checking out the guys he saw near the Ashley river bridge? Maybe he saw Tony and Ashley. Then there's Mrs. Atherton and her vicious gossip. Ashley for believing her. Annabelle for scolding him for believing. And you and I for daring to take a moment for ourselves."

Jeb paused, drew a rasping breath, and spoke a damning truth. "Most of all, it comes down to me. If it makes it easier to assign guilt, Nicky, consider where it really belongs."

Nicole turned a stony face to him. Her gaze moved to the bulky bandage at his arm, trailed over the torn shirt marked by his blood and Ashley's. At last her gaze climbed to his face, registering somewhere in her subconscious the fine lines about his eyes, his fatigue and pallor. He'd lost enough blood that he shouldn't be on his feet, but she didn't understand that. Not yet.

"All right," she said, more to appease him than in belief. "We did this to Ashley. Tony, you and I." Damning words, words he wanted. But words that weren't true, for she knew who was at fault.

She, only she, had drawn a killer to the island. Only she had disappointed a friend. Only she had fallen in love with Jeb Tanner.

Her tired, shocked mind lost the thread of coherence, skittering away to an impossible dream. "You and I," she whispered. "Jeb and Nicole."

He didn't understand, he couldn't. "Nicky..."

"Go away, Jeb," she interrupted hoarsely. "Don't make this any harder than it is."

His shoulders tensed as if she'd struck him. He lifted a hand to touch her, then knew he mustn't. "All right, Nicky, if that's what you want."

Rising, he backed away. He'd come to help, to undo what harm he could. Even that was hopeless. The sooner he was gone from her life, the better. But he couldn't go, yet. She might need him one more time.

He didn't speak to her, or go near her again. A subdued Annabelle arrived, with the laconic Harry in tow. Mitch waited by the door. Matthew was never too far from Jeb's distant seat. An eternity later, a surgeon stepped into the waiting room, searching the expectant faces. When he found Nicole's bleak gaze, he smiled.

Ashley would recover.

Amid the quiet celebration, Jeb slipped away unnoticed. As he left the hospital, the dawn had come and the day had begun.

His work was done. Simon would finish up here, with the aid of the *Gambler*'s crew.

Time to go.

There were children playing. He heard their laughter long before he climbed the stairs to the top of the dune. For what seemed the ten-thousand-and-second time, he asked himself why he was here.

He knew why.

Beneath the small shelter that covered the landing, he scanned the shore. It seemed it had been forever since he'd looked out at this sandy beach. Forever since he'd kissed a hurting woman, and held her at the crest of the ruin.

A gull wheeled by, riding a breeze. To the sound of squeals and giggles, a mischievous wave washed away an intricate maze of castles and moats built of sand. A child, a little girl, with hair like a raven's wings, dashed into the surf and was dragged back, laughing and squirming, by an older man.

No, an older kid.

"Ashley." Jeb discovered he was smiling. Stepping over a wooden railing, and breaking every rule of shoreline conservation, he tramped across the ridge of the dune. In a thicket of sea oats he found a place where he could watch unnoticed. Hunkering down in the sand, he resumed his vigil.

He lost track of time, a rare happening for Jeb. For once, he didn't care. It was hard to care when the self-appointed guardian of the little ones was having the time of his life.

Finally, in the capricious custom of early April, mild midday heat gave way to a threat of rain. Sunbathing mothers, who had been only too comfortable leaving their toddlers in Ashley's care, collected beach sheets, lounge chairs and reluctant children, and scurried away.

It was time Jeb left, as well. He'd seen what he'd come to see, heard what he wanted to hear. For months he'd kept informed from a distance, but he wanted, no, he'd needed to see first hand.

He'd needed to see that Ashley was well and happy. He'd needed to hear the laughter of the woman who sat at the base of the ruin.

He hadn't let himself think of her. After first glance, he hadn't risked a second look. But the image of the familiar, faded swimsuit with its matching shirt was etched indelibly in his memory.

Jeb climbed to his feet, time to go again.

Sand shifted and slid beneath his feet, fine granules stung his face. He looked to the horizon, storm clouds seethed at its edge. A squall was building over the sea.

"Jeb."

He looked down, surprised that Ashley stood at the base of the dune, but stunned that he remembered. "Hello, Ashley."

"My beach." He thumped his bare chest, oblivious of the scar that curved over it. His grin was warm, amiable.

Jeb looked at the ruin. Nicole had left her post. "Sure," he said softly, "I suppose it should be."

Ashley launched into a rambling monologue, complete with expansive gestures. Jeb had never heard him so vocal, nor so animated. And he didn't understand a word.

"He's saying thank you, Jeb."

Nicole had climbed the steps, she stood not an arm's length from him. She'd worn no hat today and her hair was tousled, her skin flushed from the sun, her level gaze was at peace. Her fragrance, blended with the scent of the sea, drifted on the breeze. An intoxicating mix that stirred an old need, one that never really left him.

She was so beautiful, and so close, all he needed to do to draw her into his arms was reach out. His fists clenched on an impulse so strong he barely recalled he'd thrown away the right to hold her.

He'd been fool enough without making a greater one of himself. Pretending that it hadn't been months of agony since he'd seen her, and that Jeb Tanner, master spy, hadn't been caught spying, he asked, "Why would he thank me, Nicky?"

"For the same things I could thank you for. That I *should* have thanked you for months ago. My life and Ashley's. A sense of belonging, at last." Her gaze swept over him. He looked brawny and healthy, but the fire had gone from him. He seemed jaded and world weary. She missed the zeal, the passion, the smile that turned his harsh features magnificently handsome.

The months since August had been a healing time for her. A time of coming to terms with who she was, and what she was not. She'd learned then to accept what she couldn't change, and to assume only the guilt that was hers.

Her life was better than it had been before, but none of it had been easy. None of it would have been possible without Jeb.

Matthew counselled patience, and at last she'd understood what Jeb must resolve for himself. But patience was never more difficult than now, when she saw the still unresolved remorse in him. The need.

She'd waited for him to come to her. He had one more step to take, but not here. Not now. She backed away, beyond his reach. Beyond her own need.

"I know who I am now, and what I want," she said. "Most of all, I know where I belong. Do you know? You've traveled the world, been everywhere, done everything, but to be happy there has to be one special place for each of us. One special place where we belong.

"Where is your place, Jeb? Where do you belong?"

She backed away another step. Ashley was at her heels, frightened by the flicker of lightning and the first low growl of thunder. "I have to take Ashley home to Charleston. His aunt Patrice will be waiting. She only lent him to me for the day."

At Jeb's quick look, Nicole smiled. "He lives with her now. I'm sure you knew that, but it's more than an arrangement that works for both of them. They're the last surviving members of a family. They were alone, now they have each other. Again, thanks to you."

Patrice Blakemond, a wealthy woman so reclusive even the nosiest grandes dames of Charleston knew little or nothing of her, and Ashley? Stranger things had happened. "She accepted him?"

"Without reservation." Before he could ask anything more, she rushed on, "I won't risk coming back from Charleston in the storm. If I don't see you again, good luck."

Ashley caught at her hand, anxious to be away from the threat of the storm. With a slight pressure of her fingers and a smile, Nicole calmed him.

She waited for a new rumble of thunder to fade away. She turned once more to Jeb. Her look lingered on his haggard face. Wishing she could comfort him as easily as Ashley, she called softly, "Be happy."

Nicole wandered her garden with a distorted sense of déjà vu. Months ago, a woman had walked through the mists, savoring the last minutes before a summer squall. The time when the air was humid and fragrant with the scent of summer flowers, when the wind lay still and the city beyond the gates disappeared in the hush. Then her world had been Charleston and Kiawah.

But the woman had changed, as the season changed. Flowers bending beneath the gathering weight of the mist were flowers of spring. And her world was Jeb.

Her steps were halting over stones that wandered among the flowers. Her skirt of rich purple brushed the waxen foliage that crowded the walks of her private place. Lace trembled at her breast in the anguish of waiting. She had gambled, played Matthew's game of patience. But now that patience was strained.

Yet she was sure Jeb cared. Sure Eden hadn't been a lie. So sure . . .

The bell by the gate sent its deep notes pealing through the mist. A pretty sound that left her petrified.

Jeb would be waiting beyond the vintage iron.

Had he taken the final step that meant commitment? Or had he come to say goodbye?

The bell sounded again, and again. An urgent demand that she come to him. Reluctant, afraid to hope, on leaden feet she moved down the walk, past crape myrtle and magnolia. At the gate, she stopped, stared. In the hours since she'd left him, he'd fought a battle, and every skirmish had marked him. His hair was tousled, far more than from the wind. Lines at his forehead were deeper, furrows bracketing his mouth harsher, circles beneath his eyes darker. The eyes glaring at her over graceful iron work were blazing.

"Open the gate, Nicky. Open it, or I'll tear the damned thing off its hinges."

With shaking fingers she dealt with the latch. When she would have opened it, he was there before her. Iron battered against brick with a metallic clang. Before the echo died, his hands were in her hair, lifting her face to his. She had a second to think how desperate he looked, then she didn't think at all.

His mouth was fierce against hers. His kiss was greedy, demanding, granting no quarter, accepting none. Before she could offer, he plundered. Where she would take the kiss, he went before her. He was a man adrift, she was his moor, his heart. He drank with a thirst that could be slaked, but never quenched.

When he thought he would die of wanting her, he drew away. Her face still framed in his hands, he leaned his forehead to hers. "Call me bastard and traitor, or anything unspeakable, but don't send me away, sweetheart. Please," he whispered. "Not yet."

Nicole's heart lifted. This was the fulfillment of her hopes. The last step, the end of a battle. "Never."

"I've fought this and myself and you. I've worked to exhaustion to forget, but how can I forget when my dreams won't? When every night I close my eyes they're there, waiting for me—filled with you, and lace, and this. I don't want to fight anymore, Nicky. I..." His desperately rehearsed plea faltered. "What?" He leaned away, his hands slipping to her shoulders. "What did you say?"

Lightning flickered, thunder whispered a warning. A rising wind ruffled a lock of heavy, golden hair, tumbling it over his forehead. With her fingertips she stroked it back. "I said never."

"But I lied to you."

She sighed at his determination to recount his offenses. "Did you? Tell me when."

"By omission, then, if not in fact."

"And not by choice."

"You were my Judas goat to catch Tony."

"I know, and now I understand. But Tony made me that."

"I walked away from you on Eden."

"I never expected more than we shared. A kiss isn't a covenant, Jeb, nor making love a binding promise. There were no obligations on Eden."

"Dammit! Nicky." He shook her gently. "Stop being so maddeningly reasonable."

"Would it help anything if I weren't?"

"Yes! No! It would help even more if you slapped me silly."

"I won't hit you, not ever." Leaning her cheek against his scarred arm and turning only slightly, she touched the angry blemish with her lips. "You've been hurt enough."

His breath was labored and shallow. "Nicky..."

"Don't fight me, Jeb." Lifting her head, she looked up at him. Her eyes were luminous, catching the violet of her dress and the fire of lightning. "I'd much rather you kiss me."

"Dear heaven, woman. I think before we're done, I *will* be mad." He was already drawing her to him, his head dipping to her.

"Before we're done?" she murmured against his lips. "When will that be?"

Lightning split the sky, thunder shook the ground beneath their feet. The spiraling storm gave birth to a gale that whipped their breath away, but not before she heard him promise, "Never."

Eleven

Nicole stood by a window. The sun was bright and strong. But like her, the garden bore lingering traces of a storm in the night.

Through the evening and after, rain had pounded the roof and gushed over the eaves. In the aftermath of lightning that turned the world incandescent, thunder crashed in descending darkness.

But the storm with its unbridled furor was only the minor prelude for a consuming passion.

With a contented smile she gazed out at a perfect world. In the morning light, plant and bloom had never been lovelier than when glistening with captured raindrops as they opened to the sun. She ached pleasantly in every muscle and sinew, and in her bed Jeb slept the restful sleep of absolution.

Nicole tugged her robe closer, wondering if he would ever believe there was nothing that needed forgiving. The harm was Tony's. The need to insure there would be no more children like Julie Brown transcended the cost. To her, to Jeb and even to Ashley. Now Ashley was safe, as well, thanks to Jeb.

"Good morning." Jeb slid a hand beneath her robe and drew her back against him.

Nicole smiled and let him hold her. "Hi, sleepyhead."

"Guilty." He kissed her neck. "What were you thinking?"

"About Ashley and you."

"What about us?"

"How did you know he had family nearby?"

"I played a hunch, and with a lot of help from researchers and genealogists it paid off. The best was a stroke of luck."

"The portrait of his mother at the Blakemond mansion."

"Proof positive. Only fingerprints or a battery of tests would be better."

"Patrice wouldn't hear of subjecting Ashley to them. As far as she's concerned there's no mistaking the resemblance, and his age is right. Who would ever dream the woman Folly's Castle was built for would be Ashley's mother. How could she possibly survive the hurricane that destroyed it?"

"We'll never know that part. Records tell us only that some poor, half-demented creature washed on shore miles from the island. No one knows how she eventually made her way to Charleston. Not even she remembered how or why, or even who she was. Yet she spent the rest of her life as a recluse, taking care of her baby and wandering the shore looking for something or someone."

"The castle," Nicole ventured. "And her forbidden lover."

"Maybe she had a glimmering of memory. It would explain the similarity of her real name and the surname she gave Ashley."

"She loved him, you know. He was well cared for and he'd been taught a lot. She left him the shack past the wharves and schooled him in the trade that was his livelihood after her death. He doesn't remember her and the castle can't ever really be his, but seeing it and hearing the story gives him a sense of belonging. Best of all, he has a home and a family now, for as long as he lives. Patrice is only nine years older than he. She never married and she's lonely, and Ashley can be amazingly good company." Nicole chuckled. "He's teaching her to paint."

"That's terrific." He moved the collar of her robe aside to kiss the curve of her shoulder. "You're terrific."

She turned in his arms, discovering he was delightfully naked. Rising on tiptoe she gave him a teasing kiss. "Of course I'm terrific, but not as terrific as you."

"Wanna bet?"

"Wouldn't be fair."

"How so?" With his help, her robe slipped off her shoulders.

"Because I have proof. Something you seem to have forgotten."

"When I look at you, I forget everything."

"Then you're glad you saved my life."

The robe drifted to the floor. "Very glad."

"That's it. If I'd taken your bet I would've won. You're a hero, and heroes are more terrific than anybody."

"Sweetheart." Her breast was a perfect fit for his hand.

She drew a long shuddering breath. "Hmm?"

"Hush."

"Why so quiet?" Jeb asked.

Nicole lay in his arms in the tall four-poster bed with only a sheet crumpled at her waist. She didn't answer for a long while, instead she took his hand from her breast. Linking her fingers through his, she drew their joined hands to her mouth, tracing lazy patterns over his knuckles with her lips.

Jeb didn't push, he'd begun to learn she would face any trouble. But in her own time.

When she spoke, at last, it was of Tony. "I've tried to understand what happened, and when it began. I can't believe he never loved me."

There was no answer for what happened. Part of it was that something was missing in him from the beginning. An absence of conscience that set the stage for the rest. Jeb didn't know how it happened, nor the exact moment it began. But he'd seen evidence of his detachment the day a surfboard battered his sister's face.

"He loved you. Why else did he take himself out of your life? Why did he protect you from the horror of his?" Someday, when she was ready, Jeb knew he would tell her how Tony systematically removed every trace of her connection to him. As far as the world was concerned, his sister ceased to exist shortly after she graduated from the university. When she'd turned her back on the ugliness of the academic world and relocated in the east.

There were accounts of her death, even a grave and a stone with her name on it in a cemetery in a tiny California town. A tenuous subterfuge that wouldn't have fooled the few who were close to her. But it was never intended for them. It was meant to protect her from people like the Merino family.

And it had.

"He loved you, Nicky." Jeb had seen the love, and he'd seen the beginning of its death. "He loved you very much, but through the years the demented man he became forgot."

She was quiet, thoughtful. He knew she was pondering the explanation he proposed, dissecting it, accepting it bit by bit. "I'd like to believe you." After a minute, she nodded decisively. "I choose to believe you."

It wouldn't be quite as simple as making a choice, but it was a beginning. And enough for now. Jeb kissed the top of her head, and held her tighter.

In the garden a robin sang of spring and new beginnings. Jeb was grateful for both, and pleased that Nicole was composed, and finally at ease. He let his mind drift to the past as she snuggled against him. He thought she would sleep, recouping the rest he had denied her. He was wrong.

"Now you're the quiet one."

"Am I?" he asked.

"Aren't you?" His hand was still in hers, she brought his fingers back to her kiss. "Want to tell me?"

"Nothing much to tell. I was thinking about memories. How strange they can be." He spoke as much to himself as to Nicole.

"Sometimes they are."

"Some are gone in a flash, while others are branded on our hearts and minds forever. Take you, for instance—"

She laughed. "You have."

"You asked." He kissed the top of her head. "So don't distract me by playing the wicked wanton."

"I think that's a redundant characterization, but who's playing?" she asked dryly. "And do you really want me to stop?"

His free hand drifted over her midriff, down her hip, lingering low over her stomach before inching slowly to her breast. As his caress took her breath away, he chuckled. "What would you say?"

She considered every new ache, and that he looked tired again. "I say you should continue your discourse on memory."

"Ahh, but where was I?"

"Memories are strange, and you were going to take me."

"Right." He grinned, resisted the obvious and returned to the subject virtually in midsentence. "You were a kid I knew for less than a year, but I never forgot. I remember the braces and the shy smile that tried to hide them. And the phenomenal mind.

"I had trouble with this assignment from the first. Something that hadn't happened before. Most are cut and dried, there's a problem, we solve it. That's it. But it wasn't so simple this time. I kept remembering how hard it was to be the youngest and brightest kid on campus, and how you looked when you discovered someone you trusted was only using your mind. I knew that before this was done, I would see that look again. This time, I would be the one who put it there.

"I wasn't wrong, Nicky. I saw it in the hospital, while we waited to hear if Ashley would live or die."

"So you went away, because of a look."

"Sounds crazy now, but yes."

"But you're back."

"And all is well, even with Ashley. I didn't think he would remember after so long. But he did and I could swear he was glad to see me."

"Memory is strange. Haven't you questioned why he didn't forget you?"

"It occurred to me it was unusual."

"Not so unusual when he has a photograph of you."

"Oh?" Photographs of the men of The Black Watch, of Simon's Ladies from Hell, were rare. But Nicole knew nothing of the clandestine organization. She assumed he and the men who came with him to the island were part of a unique police force. The first part, at least, was true. With Simon's permission, he would tell her what he could, when the time was right.

"Mitch brought the photograph. A snapshot, actually."

"He did?" There was surprise in Jeb's voice. "When?"

"He attended the services for Tony." Links of Jeb's bracelet pressed against the curve of her jaw as she held his hand tighter. It was ironic that Brett's gift of thanks for saving her husband's life, and hands, had saved Jeb's. Someday she would find Brett McLachlan and tell her. And thank her.

"Nicky." Jeb prodded her from her wandering thoughts. "Why the photograph?"

"Sorry, I just had a thought, something I need to do, but it can wait."

"The photograph, Nicky."

"Yes, of course, the photograph. You've seen that Ashley's memory is selective."

"I have."

"I'm afraid his clearest memory of the evening he was shot is that he hurt you with the knife when he fell. It was an accident. We understand, but he can't. For a time he was convinced you died, too. Like Tony. He couldn't deal with being responsible. Matthew suggested the photograph, to prove you were all right. Ashley knows what you've done for him, Patrice reminds him regularly. Now he won't part with your picture."

"I didn't know." An understatement. Mitch had never mentioned the services. Neither he nor Matthew ever hinted at continued contact with Nicole. But not even the fearless men of The Black Watch prodded a wolf with a sore heart.

"Matthew said you didn't want to know, that you weren't ready to deal with...everything." She turned in his arms, her body lying over his. "Most of all, he says you couldn't deal with falling in love with me."

"Matthew talks too damn much."

"Matthew says very little, and only what I need to hear."

He tugged his hand from hers, to frame the face that looked solemnly down at him. "Maybe it's time I said what you need to hear. Maybe I need to hear it myself."

Nicole waited, but he didn't continue. After an endless minute, he sighed heavily. "It isn't quite as simple as I thought. First there's something I have to explain."

She waited again, silently.

"I didn't want this assignment and I didn't want to see you again. For a lot of reasons. Added to them was the possibility you were an accessory."

"Accessory!" The word burst from her in its inherent horror.

"Shh, love. Hear me out. I said possibility. I'm alive today because I look at all the possibilities. Even the long shots."

"You thought I could..." Her voice failed. As she pulled away from him, tears she'd denied when she'd lost a brother, and nearly a friend and finally a lover, sparkled in her eyes. "What if..."

"If you were part of it? God, sweetheart, that's what was tearing me apart."

"Why? Whatever was needed would have been part of your assignment, wouldn't it? So why would you care?"

"Because I knew even before I came, that if I saw you again I would fall in love with you." He wanted to touch her, to draw her back to him and comfort her. But he knew she wouldn't accept his comfort, not yet. "I would have loved you years ago, but we were at different stages of our lives, and the timing wasn't right." A sound rumbled deep in his throat, a mix of concession and bittersweet laughter. "I didn't stand a chance the second time around."

She spun away from him, taking the sheet with her as she left the bed. Swathed in its bright color, with thumb and index finger kneading her temples, she muttered in shocked tones. "You say it was preordained that you were going to fall in love with me. Yet, if it was necessary, you were going to..."

"No."

She took her hand from her eyes, her gaze challenging his. "Then what?"

"I didn't know then. I don't now."

"Who are you?" She was shivering. "What are you?"

He left the bed and crossed the room to her. "I'm not like Tony. I'm Jeb Tanner, time hasn't changed that. What am I? A hunter, and more. Someday I'll explain. But can't it be enough, for now, that I'm a man who loves you?"

Nicole looked mutely out at the garden.

"I walked away from you before, Nicky, not because of what I am, but because I thought it was what you wanted. I will again, but this time you have to tell me to go."

She didn't respond.

"There are things I can't tell you, not ever. I'm sorry for that, but I won't lie to you, and I won't hurt you. You trusted me on Eden, and you said you loved me." Curving his palm around her cheek, he turned her unresisting face back to his. "Do you trust me now? *Will* you trust me enough to love me again?"

Could she? Her mind was whirling, but the answer wasn't in her mind. She searched her heart. The answer was there. "Yes." The tears she'd fought for so long spilled down her cheeks. "I will."

"There was a child on the beach today. A little girl with hair as black as the night. She could have been our child, Nicky. I knew then where I belonged, and how much I wanted a little girl who looks like you."

"You would spoil her."

"Shamelessly," he agreed as he traced the path of a tear to the corner of her mouth. "But most of all I would love her."

Nicole laid her palms on his chest, savoring the feel of him. Did his reason for coming to the island matter? Did anything matter when the man who had risked his life for hers looked at her as he did now? Sliding her hands up his body she rose to tease his lips with hers. "And her mother?"

"I will love you."

No frills, no window dressing, but then, heroes didn't need them.

"How long?" she whispered as he swept her into his arms where she belonged.

The hunter didn't give his heart easily. But when he did, it was...

"Forever."

* * * * *

In September, look for THE SAINT OF BOURBON STREET, *Book Two, in the Men of The Black Watch miniseries by BJ James.*

COMING NEXT MONTH

#943 THE WILDE BUNCH—Barbara Boswell

August's *Man of the Month*, rancher Mac Wilde, needed a woman to help raise his four kids. So he took Kara Kirby as his wife in name only....

#944 COWBOYS DON'T QUIT—Anne McAllister

Code of the West

Sexy cowboy Luke Tanner was trying to escape his past, and Jillian Crane was the only woman who could help him. Unfortunately she also happened to be the woman he was running from....

#945 HEART OF THE HUNTER—BJ James

Men of the Black Watch

Fifteen years ago, Jeb Tanner had mysteriously disappeared from Nicole Callison's life. Now the irresistible man had somehow found her, but how could Nicole be sure his motives for returning were honorable?

#946 MAN OVERBOARD—Karen Leabo

Private investigator Harrison Powell knew beautiful Paige Stovall was hiding something. But it was too late—she had already pushed him overboard...with desire!

#947 THE RANCHER AND THE REDHEAD—Susannah Davis

The only way Sam Preston could keep custody of his baby cousin was to marry. So he hoodwinked Roni Daniels into becoming his wife!

#948 TEXAS TEMPTATION—Barbara McCauley

Hearts of Stone

Jared Stone was everything Annie Bailey had ever wanted in a man, but he was the one man she could *never* have. Would she risk the temptation of loving him when everything she cared about was at stake?

MILLION DOLLAR SWEEPSTAKES (III)

No purchase necessary. To enter, follow the directions published. Method of entry may vary. For eligibility, entries must be received no later than March 31, 1996. No liability is assumed for printing errors, lost, late or misdirected entries. Odds of winning are determined by the number of eligible entries distributed and received. Prizewinners will be determined no later than June 30, 1996.

Sweepstakes open to residents of the U.S. (except Puerto Rico), Canada, Europe and Taiwan who are 18 years of age or older. All applicable laws and regulations apply. Sweepstakes offer void wherever prohibited by law. Values of all prizes are in U.S. currency. This sweepstakes is presented by Torstar Corp., its subsidiaries and affiliates, in conjunction with book, merchandise and/or product offerings. For a copy of the Official Rules send a self-addressed, stamped envelope (WA residents need not affix return postage) to: MILLION DOLLAR SWEEPSTAKES (III) Rules, P.O. Box 4573, Blair, NE 68009, USA.

EXTRA BONUS PRIZE DRAWING

No purchase necessary. The Extra Bonus Prize will be awarded in a random drawing to be conducted no later than 5/30/96 from among all entries received. To qualify, entries must be received by 3/31/96 and comply with published directions. Drawing open to residents of the U.S. (except Puerto Rico), Canada, Europe and Taiwan who are 18 years of age or older. All applicable laws and regulations apply; offer void wherever prohibited by law. Odds of winning are dependent upon number of eligible entries received. Prize is valued in U.S. currency. The offer is presented by Torstar Corp., its subsidiaries and affiliates in conjunction with book, merchandise and/or product offering. For a copy of the Official Rules governing this sweepstakes, send a self-addressed, stamped envelope (WA residents need not affix return postage) to: Extra Bonus Prize Drawing Rules, P.O. Box 4590, Blair, NE 68009, USA.

SWP-S895

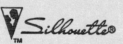

As a *Privileged Woman,*
you'll be entitled to all these *Free Benefits.*
And *Free Gifts,* too.

To thank you for buying our books, we've designed an exclusive FREE program called *PAGES & PRIVILEGES™.* You can enroll with just one Proof of Purchase, and get the kind of luxuries that, until now, you could only read about.

BIG HOTEL DISCOUNTS

A privileged woman stays in the finest hotels. And so can you—at up to 60% off! Imagine standing in a hotel check-in line and watching as the guest in front of you pays $150 for the same room that's only costing you $60. Your *Pages & Privileges* discounts are good at Sheraton, Marriott, Best Western, Hyatt and thousands of other fine hotels all over the U.S., Canada and Europe.

FREE DISCOUNT TRAVEL SERVICE

A privileged woman is always jetting to romantic places. When you fly, just make one phone call for the lowest published airfare at time of booking—or double the difference back! PLUS— you'll get a $25 voucher to use the first time you book a flight AND 5% cash back on every ticket you buy thereafter through the travel service!

SD-PP4A

ℱREE GIFTS!

A privileged woman is always getting wonderful gifts.
Luxuriate in rich fragrances that will stir your senses (and his). This gift-boxed assortment of fine perfumes includes three popular scents, each in a beautiful designer bottle.   Truly Lace...This luxurious fragrance unveils your sensuous side. L'Effleur...discover the romance of the Victorian era with this soft floral. Muguet des bois...a single note floral of singular beauty.

YOURS FREE!

$50 VALUE

ℱREE INSIDER TIPS LETTER

A privileged woman is always informed. And you'll be, too, with our free letter full of fascinating information and sneak previews of upcoming books.

ℳORE GREAT GIFTS & BENEFITS TO COME

A privileged woman always has a lot to look forward to. And so will you. You get all these wonderful FREE gifts and benefits now with only one purchase...and there are no additional purchases required. However, each additional retail purchase of Harlequin and Silhouette books brings you a step closer to even more great FREE benefits like half-price movie tickets... and even more FREE gifts.

L'Effleur...This basketful of romance lets you discover L'Effleur from head to toe, heart to home.

Truly Lace... A basket spun with the sensuous luxuries of Truly Lace, including Dusting Powder in a reusable satin and lace covered box.

Complete the Enrollment Form in the front of this book and mail it with this Proof of Purchase.

| 📖 PROOF OF PURCHASE |
| Offer expires October 31, 1996 |

SD-PP4